SEEING IS DECEIVING

You are so there.

TWITCHES

T•WITCHES

H.B. GILMOUR
& RANDI REISFELD

SCHOLASTIC
NEW YORK   TORONTO   LONDON   AUCKLAND   SYDNEY
MEXICO CITY   NEW DELHI   HONG KONG   BUENOS AIRES

ISBN 0-439-24072-7

12 11 10 9 8 7 6 5 4 3 2 1   1 2 3 4 5 6/0

PRINTED IN THE U.S.A.
FIRST SCHOLASTIC PRINTING, DECEMBER 2001

DEDICATION

Dedicated to the memory of Deanna Reisfeld.
Thanks for the inspiration, the support,
and the red-haired twins.
—R.R.

With love and gratitude, for PJ and Fred.
—H.B.G.

A SPECIAL SHOUT OUT

THE AUTHORS WOULD LIKE TO
SEND A SPECIAL WHOO-HOO! TO
STEVE KASDIN, NATHANIEL
BISSON, MICHELLE LEWY, ELLIE
BERGER, TINA MCINTYRE, AND
THEIR TEAMS FOR USING THEIR
EXTREMELY EXCELLENT GIFTS ON
BEHALF OF T*WITCHES.

CHAPTER ONE
THE SHOPLIFTER

Snap! It happened in a heartbeat. So fast, no one could have seen it. No one normal, that is.

Camryn hadn't seen it yet, but she was about to. If not for the sudden attack of icy chills and the dizzying headache stopping her in her tracks, she might not have bothered to look around. But by now, she knew that the strange sensations that had been coming over her since childhood always warned of something.

Like now. Like right here, in the middle of the Jewelry Corner, at the Marble Bay Galleria. Something bad was about to happen.

Behind her.

Cam whirled around. Across the store, she saw a girl about her own age, with stringy brown hair, trembling, reaching out toward the case where the most expensive jewelry was locked. The kind of jewelry that a salesperson had to extract for the customer to look at, to try on. Out on that counter, on a plush velvet cushion, sat a sparkling diamond tennis bracelet. But only for a split second.

Cam narrowed her intense gray eyes. In addition to her ability to sense things before they happened, Cam also had incredible powers of sight. She telescoped in on the scene. A tall, thin woman with brassy blond hair was standing next to the girl and drew the salesperson's attention away. In that instant, the girl quickly swiped the sparkler and slipped it into the right-hand pocket of her peacoat — in the same motion, she reached into her left-hand pocket, withdrew a look-alike bracelet, and replaced the one she'd stolen. The action had taken a fraction of a second.

Although she'd been at the other end of the store and shouldn't have been able to see any of it Camryn Barnes had just witnessed a shoplifting.

In another corner of the store, the scent hit Alex before she heard the words. Fetid, sweaty, sticky, the smell of fear. Like Camryn, Alex had hyperabilities. She could smell things that regular people couldn't. She could hear things, too. Even things that people thought, but didn't say, like the unspoken pleas of a girl. *Please don't make me do this! It's wrong.... I'll get caught.... I don't want to....*

Behind her.

Alex Fielding realized the panicked thoughts were coming from the other end of the store.

Another voice, this one scratchy, older, female, also unspoken: *She'd better hurry it up! This kid is so slow — where'd we get her from, anyway? We've gone over this drill a thousand times. Just pick up the bracelet and stick it in your pocket, and replace it with the one we brought. We really need this!*

Alex knew what she had to do.

Bolting to the jewelry case, she wasn't surprised to find her identical twin sister also on the way. Cam had clearly seen what Alex had heard. No words passed between the twins as they gained on the thieves, who were now halfway to the exit.

Cam intercepted them, blocking their way. Before the robbers realized her move was deliberate, Alex was by her side.

The woman wore big sunglasses and was clearly rattled. With long, thin pincerlike arms, she tried to elbow past the twin-barrier. "Excuse me! Out of the way!"

"Not so fast," Cam said evenly. "Did you leave something behind at the jewelry counter?"

Cam could see through the sunglasses. The woman's black bug eyes flashed daggers at her. "No, we did not." Her voice riveted Cam. Scratchy and harsh, she hissed, "We're in a hurry. Now move!"

Her own huge, inky-gray eyes flashing, Cam stared her down. "Not until you return what you stole."

The woman didn't react, but the girl was in full-tilt panic, her whole body trembling. Alex's heart went out to her. Whatever heist this duo was pulling off, the girl had been pushed into it.

Reflexively, the girl's hand went to her pocket, and her jaw dropped. "How . . . how did you . . . ?" she sputtered.

The woman whirled on the girl. "Lizzie! Just tell them you didn't steal anything. Let's go!"

Lizzie bit her lip and started to shake. "I . . . you . . ."

"You know she did!" Cam seethed — the pair were in this together! What kind of mother would force her own daughter to steal? "I saw you distract the saleswoman so she could make the switch! How can you —"

Alex's sharp kick to her shins stopped Cam's rant. *Give me a sec,* she telepathically communicated to her twin.

Then Alex leaned over to the girl and whispered,

"Let go of the bracelet for a minute. I'm going to help you."

As the woman began to protest, Cam stared hard at her, using her powers to stun.

It worked — the sunglasses were no shield against Cam's remarkable gray eyes. The woman became confused and froze for a minute.

Alex went into action.

"Come back to the counter with me," she directed Lizzie. "Let's be casual."

"No! I can't. . . . I didn't want to. Please don't turn me in."

"Sssshh, trust me," Alex whispered as she escorted the terrified girl back to the scene of the crime. "Just pretend we're friends checking out the baubles. Stand next to me. Keep both hands in front of you, on the counter. Don't touch anything."

Petrified now, Lizzie did as she was told.

The saleswoman was at the register and had her back to the counter. It wouldn't be long before she turned around, however. That was all Alex needed.

Let this work, Alex prayed silently.

Alex focused on the jewelry in Lizzie's pocket. She pictured the bracelet drifting up and saw it settling neatly onto the countertop. Alex was just beginning to be comfortable with her powers — like this one, the ability to move objects just by thinking about them. She waited, fully expecting to hear the gentle clink of diamonds on glass.

Instead, she heard nothing. What was she doing wrong?

In school, when a jock had picked on a mentally challenged kid, Alex had loosened the drawstring on his sweatpants — somehow they'd fallen down, right in the middle of a basketball game. That was one for the yearbook!

And just the other day, she'd found a rusted nail and given a sudden flat tire to a road-rageful driver who'd blasted through a stop sign.

She'd been angry. Is that what it would take to help this girl? Well, she'd work up a righteous fury, then!

It didn't take much. Alex had just heard that this girl was being forced into stealing. She glanced at the flustered woman Cam had immobilized. What kind of twisted adult used a kid to steal a . . .

Bracelet! At that moment, Lizzie gasped. The diamond bracelet came wafting out of her pocket, as if buffeted by a gentle breeze, and landed gently on the counter, barely making a sound.

Mission accomplished.

Alex grabbed Lizzie's bony arm and rushed her out of the store. The blond woman went flying in another direction.

"We did it! Go, us!" Although her head still ached, Cam was flushed with excitement. "How cool was that? We totally prevented a robbery! Probably, we just saved another young soul from a life of crime, made her really think about her actions, that crime so does not pay." Jubilant, Cam raised her palm for Alex to slap.

"Kudos overload, anyone?" Alex said grumpily, ignoring her twin's hand. "We saw, we heard, we intercepted. After that brief commercial break, they'll probably just rob another store. So don't get all PAX-TV."

"What crawled up your caboose?" Cam demanded.

"It wasn't the girl, and you know it," Alex replied. "The woman pushed her to do it, and in that little drama, we probably had a negative effect."

Cam paused. She did know. But she realized Alex knew more. "You heard their thoughts, didn't you? What were they?"

"The woman was insisting, 'We really need this.'" Alex stopped.

"They *need* it? That's so weird. They were well-dressed, they're not the type —"

"What's 'the type,' Camryn? What would you know about the 'type' of people who steal? Are you saying only poor people steal?"

As she always did, Cam took the bait and got defensive. "Gee, thanks, Als, I so need a reminder of your humble roots, which, of course, equals the 'good' twin; versus my privileged upbringing, which equals the 'bad' twin. I mean, the last seventy-nine zillion zingers just weren't enough."

Unrepentant, Alex stuck out her chin. "Sorry if our life experiences were on the unparallel bars. When it came to the adoption lottery, could *you* help it if your number turned up among the big-bucks Barnes clan? Yet somehow, you managed to make do — the big house, trendy togs, laptop, cell phone, the trinkets of the trendoids. I know, it wasn't easy. . . ."

Cam grimaced and wound the chain of her sun necklace around her finger tightly. The headaches she suffered after her premonitions lingered. Now Alex was giving her a bigger one.

"Oh, and BTW," Alex added. "Shoplifter woman? Not that girl's mom."

The twins, identical in their pouty lips, gently sloped noses, strong jaws, and intense, charcoal-rimmed gray eyes, were opposite in just about everything else. Including:

Dress: Cam was neatly pressed Banana Republic/ Gap girl; Alex, the draggy, baggy crop-topper.

'Do: Cam's thick chestnut hair brushed her shoulders; Alex's gelled spikes stood at attention, in stripes of auburn, scarlet, and blue.

Demeanor: Cam was naturally upbeat and sunny; Alex usually introspective and moody.

Only now, they were both grouchy. They glared at each other.

For the subject of mothers was a sore one. And a major one. Clarification: the most major one.

Camryn Barnes and Alexandra Fielding had been raised by different families, in different parts of the country. Cam grew up in the upscale suburb of Marble Bay, Massachusetts, with Dave and Emily Barnes. Alex grew up in rural Crow Creek, Montana, with her mom, Sara Fielding. The girls never knew they were adopted. Never knew they were twins. Never knew they were witches, really.

Until last summer, only a few short months ago. The summer they accidentally met, the summer that changed their lives forever. Alex and Camryn learned the truth about themselves — or at least part of it. They learned that they were born Artemis and Apolla into an illustrious family of witches and warlocks. They discovered that their biological father was dead and that they had been separated at birth to prevent evil witches and warlocks from harming them. But of their mother, they knew nothing beyond her name: Miranda. Who she really was, where she was, or even *if* she was — alive or dead.

In the middle of finding all of this out, Alex's mom, Sara, died. Which is how Alex came to live with Cam's family. Together, the twins had been trying to piece together who they were, what their powers were, and what they were destined to do with them.

Now the twins walked silently through the mall. After a while Cam blurted, "We should have reported them. You're right. They'll probably just go into another store and steal something else."

"Reported them?" Alex rolled her intense silvery eyes. "And said exactly what? Here's the thing, Officer. See, we're witches. And in that witch capacity, I can sometimes hear what people are thinking. And my sister here? Who was in the earring section, with her back turned? Her special witchy gift includes premonitions and abnormally sharp sight, so she eyewitnessed the heist from twenty feet away. Slammin' plan, Cam-era."

Cam winced. She so hated when Alex did that mocking thing. Especially when Als was, like, right. She folded her arms. "What's *your* action plan, then?"

"Inaction."

"Inaction," Cam repeated. "So brilliant, yet so bone-headed!"

"What part of 'we do nothing' don't you understand?" Alex challenged, leaning into Cam. "We're . . ." She lowered her voice. "Witches. Not cops. We only flat-lined the robbery because of the girl. She was forced to steal. But we probably only made it worse for her."

Cam's head was still throbbing, no thanks to Alex. "Okay, look, you're probably right. I . . ."

Alex grew concerned. "What's the matter? You don't look so good."

"I'm feelin' woozy. You go ahead, I'm going to CVS."

"Want me to come?" Alex offered.

She didn't, really. Besides headache relief, she wanted Alex relief. So what if identi-girl was often on target? Big deal — Alex had all the right questions, but none of the answers.

And Cam just needed not to see her own face belligerently staring at her. Head down, she hurried toward the mall drugstore. As she hurtled around the nearest corner, she checked over her shoulder to be sure Alex wasn't following her.

Bad plan. She crashed full-on into a freestanding cart. . . .

"Whoa! Hey . . . Watch out!"

. . . And ricocheted right into the boy who was working at it.

CHAPTER TWO
HELPING HANDS

"Extraordinary tackle!" The boy was obviously shaken — but not stirred enough to be angry with her. Which was lucky, considering Cam had clumsily managed to knock them both to the ground!

Cam turned crimson and managed a weak, "I'm so sorry! I can't believe I just did that."

"And yet, it appears you did," he said teasingly, starting to get up. He was obviously unhurt. But when Cam didn't respond right away, he added, "Hey, crash-test, are you okay?"

She shook her head and focused, finally locking eyes with the boy she'd body-slammed. His were the color of cocoa, a light milky chocolate. His tousled hair was the same color.

Cam's hands went clammy. Her heart began to pound, she could feel her cheeks start to burn — and strangely, goose bumps rose at the back of her neck. It felt less like a premonition, more like a powerful attraction to the hottie she'd just knocked over. Because, on a scale of one to studliness, this boy was, she chuckled inwardly at the expression that came to her, knock-down-drag-out off the charts.

Cam dusted herself off. "Only my pride is bruised, thanks. I am so embarrassed!" She reached out, assuming he'd extended his hand to help her up.

Assumption wrong.

Instead, he bent to pick up her tote, which she'd dropped during the head-on. It was when they were both standing that she noticed how tall he was, easily over six feet. Her eye level was at his chest, on which he wore an unusual pin, in the shape of a hand. It read, I'M SHANE. ASK ME ABOUT HELPING HANDS.

He laughed, seeing her staring at the pin. "Yes, I am."

"Uh . . . you're what?" Another clever retort, Cam bemoaned. That's flustered — one; composure — zero.

"Shane Wright. That's my name. And you would be . . ."

"Cam." Flushed, she amended, "That is, Camryn Barnes."

"Well, 'That Is Camryn Barnes,'" he teased, "I wasn't expecting you to plow into me, but I'm glad you did."

"You're glad?" Okay, off to an improbable start, but he was totally flirting.

"Sure . . . now you have to give me your full attention. You owe me."

Or not.

Cam frowned. Shane, devastatingly cute as he was, was selling something. He probably only considered Cam a customer — and a klutz! She took in the freestanding cart he was working at. It was packed with books and pamphlets, all with the same distinctive logo.

"Helping Hands is a new organization. We raise money for kids in need," the boy was explaining earnestly, as if Cam hadn't just plowed into him.

"Like UNICEF?" Cam asked, still trying to regain her composure.

"Sort of, but more focused. We run Sunshine House, which is a shelter for kids who've been abused and abandoned or living below the poverty level. You'd be surprised how many kids fall into that category."

Cam flashed on Alex. Her twin had certainly been part of *that* statistic, living in a tin trailer, her critically ill mom working two minimum-wage jobs. If she'd only known Alex back then, she could have helped. How grossly unfair that they'd been separated.

"Needy children, huh? You managed that in record time!" Alex had followed her after all. And, thanks a lot, managed to break up her moment with Shane.

Double take. That's what usually happened when people saw Cam and Alex together for the first time. Coupled with some lame attempt at a clever comment like, "Are you twins?"

Not this time. Seeing Alex approach got no such response from Shane. Helping Hands boy merely changed his sales tactic. With a terse, "Take a pamphlet, or two — and call if you're interested in signing up," he turned his attention to another potential volunteer.

Annoyed, Cam said to Alex, "What are you talking about?"

Alex shrugged and nodded at the Helping Hands cart. "I remind you how privileged you are, and feeling guilty, you run to some volunteer organization. Predictable much, Camryn?"

Cam shot back, "Swing and a miss, Derek Jeter. I did not feel guilty, and as for this" — she motioned to the cart — "in my burning need to get away from you, I accidentally bumped into this cart. It wasn't here last week."

"You would know. Mall-crawler that you are." Alex then pointed up the aisle at someone. "Speaking of which, isn't that your other shopping half?"

Striding toward them was a more-than-familiar figure. Tall and angular Beth Fish, Cam's BFF — best friend forever. Her wiry bronze hair fanning out in all directions, Beth usually wore a smile on her good-natured freckled face.

Not now.

As she came upon the twins, she tried but failed to hide her feelings. "I'm surprised to see you here, Cam. Didn't you say you were doing homework all day?"

For the second time in five minutes, Cam was embarrassed; she'd totally blown it. Beth *had* called earlier to suggest a mall troll. But at the time, Cam was all about writing her social studies paper. Which she really had thought would take all day.

Except it hadn't. And when Dave, her dad (OK, "adoptive dad" now), had offered her and Alex a ride to the mall, they'd accepted. Dave had reminded the girls that Emily's birthday wasn't far off, and he knew Cam would want to get a gift for her mom.

Cam had forgotten that Beth had asked her to go earlier. And now it was worse than a simple disconnect. Seeing Alex, Beth probably assumed that Cam had wanted to just be with her sister, and had purposely left Beth out.

Cam owned her bad and tried to explain. "It was so last minute. My mom's birthday is coming up, my dad had to go to the office and offered us a ride —"

Beth obviously didn't believe Cam. "Lose the excuses, Camryn. I just didn't expect to see you, that's all. FYI: After all these years, I think I know when your mom's birthday is."

Whatever Alex said now wouldn't help, but she tried anyway. "Eyewitness, that's how it went down."

"Speaking of what just went down," Cam piped up a little too quickly, "you so will not believe it! We were just in the Jewelry Corner and saw this shoplifting."

Beth's eyebrows shot up. "No way! What happened? What'd you do?"

Exactly what are you about to tell her? Alex's thoughts soared into Cam's brain like a paper airplane. *Same story you were about to tell the police?*

Cam giggled nervously and backpedaled. "I mean, it looked like this girl . . . was sorta being pushed by this woman . . . to like . . . steal this bracelet."

Miffed, because she knew she was being left out again, Beth shook her head. "You're being weird. Which so defines you these days."

Weird was understating it, and Cam knew it. Since they'd met in grade school, she'd been able to tell Beth anything, everything. And vice versa. Their trust in each other had been total and complete. "Friends till the end," they always said, locking pinkies when they were young. Now everything was different. There was very little that Cam could tell Beth about the truth, about her past. And this had created a rift between the two best friends. It felt like there was little Cam could do about it.

But Beth could. Deliberately turning away from the twins, she picked up a brochure from the cart, feigning mega-interest in the Helping Hands info. Shane promptly fixed his attention on her. "Hi, can I take a minute of your time to tell you about . . ." Beth flashed him a shy smile. And told him she had plenty of time. And would love to listen.

Cam stood watching, feeling foolish. Should she insert herself into their convo? After all, she'd bumped into Shane first . . . not that this was about a cute guy! Besides, now that they had met up, the three of them should hang together. She took a step toward Beth.

But Alex grabbed her elbow and pulled her back, whispering, "Beth doesn't want you hanging with her right this minute."

"How would you know? Don't tell me — she was thinking that!"

"I did not have to hear her thoughts to know her pride is hurt," Alex whispered as she forced Cam to walk away with her. "You didn't mean to, but you dissed her.

Now she's acting like she's got better things to do. Let her. You'll make it up to her tomorrow at school. Besides, you still don't have a present for Emily."

"*We* don't have a present," Cam corrected Alex. It was the only correction required. In terms of everything else her twin had said? Straight up. Alex was right. Again.

Which did not resuscitate Cam's mood. The girl who "drank sunlight for breakfast," as Alex sometimes thought, was acting like a dark cloud was hanging over her. And as much as Alex felt like letting Cam brood . . . she couldn't. "Let it go," she advised. "You and Beth have been on the outs before. Forgive and forget, isn't that what you two are all about?"

Cam sighed. "I guess. It's just that something feels different this time."

"Different how?"

"Als . . . if you had tapped into her thoughts and there *was* something else, you would tell me, right?"

Alex gave her twin a look. "I told you. I did not listen to her thoughts. And you know exactly why. We're not supposed to use our powers to eavesdrop —"

"Or pick up gossip, or even soothe hurt friends. That's not what they're for," Cam finished Alex's sentence. "I know."

As the twins ambled through the mall, Alex softened. "Look, you're probably right. When Beth called this afternoon, what exactly did she say?"

Cam hit rewind. What Beth had said was, "I need to go to the mall. Come with?" When Cam had declined, Beth added urgently, "I really need to get out of the house."

She had not asked Beth why.

CHAPTER THREE
A CRISIS ON COVENTRY ISLAND

From her lakeside bungalow on Conventry Island, the beautiful young witch Ileana sensed strife between the girls. Attuned to them, she knew when they were simply upset — *and* when they were in real danger. She'd certainly known them long enough.

Fifteen years ago, Ileana had been given responsibility for the infant twins, all but orphaned at birth. Their father, Aron, had been brutally slain by his brother, the evil warlock Thantos, and the twins' mother had been disposed of, leaving the babies helpless and alone. The Unity Council, the ruling body of Coventry Island, had named Ileana guardian as a way of instilling responsibility in the obstinate young witch. Perhaps not coincidentally, Ileana was an orphan herself.

But she'd been a teenager then, and her own guardian, Karsh, had helped her. Who was she kidding? Ileana chewed her fingernails and obsessively braided and unbraided her long flaxen hair. Boris, her orange tabby, regarded her suspiciously from his perch on the window seat. Lord Karsh had done all the work, knowing the infants had to be separated, or their evil uncle Thantos would deal them the same fate as their parents.

Karsh had found safe homes for them, protectors to bring them up. For the next fourteen years, while Ileana tended to herself, Karsh dutifully tracked them, subconsciously guided them as they grew. No one had tried to harm them, no evil forces had even found them.

Until the day they met and came to live together.

They became targets. The relentless Thantos would not give up until he got what he wanted. And he wanted the twins.

Ileana had been called to active duty, not only protecting and safeguarding the fledglings, but guiding them in the proper uses of their developing powers. At first Ileana had been resentful of the responsibility thrust upon her. But once she'd accepted it, she decided to excel at it. Be better than Karsh at it.

That grandiosity is exactly what led her into the mess she was in now.

The young witch was in deep trouble. And though she'd never show it, scared. Terrified, down to the tips of her Jimmy Choo sandals and furiously fuschia pedicured toenails. A fear that was as paralyzing as it was foreign. She hated it.

But what she hated more was the creeping suspicion that her own stubborn willfulness was at the rotten root of it. Ileana had never been one to doubt herself. But this time, she had a sinking feeling that she had gone too far. That her own burning need to be brilliant, to show off, to be best and first, coupled with her impatience, was a potent and poisonous mix. Toxic enough, possibly, to doom the one person she loved and needed most.

Karsh was missing. The ancient tracker, her guardian, protector, and teacher; the man who'd been both father and mother to her — the safety net who was always there, no matter how much she misbehaved — was gone.

Kidnapped.

Exactly when he had been taken, Ileana didn't know. She'd been busy, how could she know? After bailing the impetuous twins, Apolla and Artemis — Camryn and Alexandra, as they were now known — out of their latest misadventure, she'd had serious catching up to do.

Corresponding via e-mail with Brice Stanley, the movie star she now knew to be a warlock; tending to her fabulous herb garden; pouring over the latest style magazines and catalogs that had piled up in her absence; and maybe a little crowing to the other witches in her circle.

She'd earned bragging rights for her latest escapade, bringing a suspected criminal to face the Unity Council. Why shouldn't everyone on Coventry Island know it? Okay, so she'd been a little self-absorbed, what was the harm in that? Hence, it was possible that a week, maybe more, had gone by before she realized she hadn't seen Karsh. But the idea that Lord Karsh, esteemed and respected, canny, learned, brilliant — but also slowed and bent by age — was in trouble would never have crossed her seamless brow.

Then the e-mails started arriving.

"We have him," the first one said.

"Who are you, and who've you got?" she typed back, annoyed at the random IM that had broken into her real-time cyberchat with Brice.

"You know the answers, Ileana," came the response.

So they knew her name. She would not panic. Even though her e-mail address did not include any elements of her name. She canceled the bothersome IM.

Then the next one came.

He has a message for you: his compliments on

your most recent transmutation. But for some reason, he insists on calling you "grumpy goddess." We surely don't know why, but you probably do.

Only one person would be proud of her transmutation. The same person who *affectionately* called her "grumpy goddess." Karsh.

Frantically, she'd tried to summon her aged mentor. He didn't respond to her phone calls or telepathic messages. She'd even trekked across the heavily wooded island to the old man's cabin. Finding it empty, she'd tracked down his cronies, Exalted Elders like Lord Grivveniss, Lady Iolande, the Lords Persiphus and Gordian, casually inquiring whether they'd seen him lately. No one had. Not wanting to alarm them, she'd breezily announced, "Then he must still be on the mainland. I'll find him there."

When she'd returned, another e-mail was waiting: His wrists are bound, his legs caught in chains. He can cast no spell to free himself; he is powerless against us. Only you can help him, brave and imperious Ileana!

To which she'd furiously typed, What do you want from me?

Instantly, the message came back: Come and get him. If you dare!

Okay, I'll play, she'd gamely responded. Where are you holding him?

Surely the brilliant Ileana can figure it out. P.S.: Make it fast.

And then, an addendum: He won't last long.

Picturing her beloved guardian in pain terrified her. Karsh was a master of the craft — still, even he would be no match for those who had him. The messages were unsigned, but she knew who they were from.

Lord Thantos, that brutal murderer — her sworn enemy — and no doubt, his skanky messenger, the despicable Fredo.

It was to the last one that she owed the mess she was in now.

She paced her lushly carpeted bungalow by the lake, trying to piece everything together. Surely, a brilliant solution would come to her. But every time she mentally finished the puzzle, the picture was the same. She'd messed up. Big time.

Only a few weeks ago, Fredo had tried to capture Apolla and Artemis. She'd come to the rescue, picked him up by his scruffy neck, and flown him back to Coventry Island.

"I'm a remarkable goddess," she'd bragged to Karsh. "Even Lady Rhianna was impressed. I dropped Fredo on the Council's doorstep. They'd been trying to get him for years — as an accessory to something or other."

Karsh had asked, "Did Lady Rhianna explain his crime?"

Haughtily, Ileana had responded, "Did I care? I was so eager to rid myself of that putrid package, I just left him with her. . . ."

Ping! That was the moment. She'd left him with a single Elder alone. And broken the rules. "A suspected criminal, when brought in, is not to be left with fewer than three Elders in attendance." She should have waited until Lady Potato (as Ileana called her) had summoned two more.

Instead, Ileana had impatiently flown away, carried on the wings of egotism.

And Fredo had escaped.

Now, the cowardly lyin' warlock and his mastermind had Karsh.

The trap had been set. They knew she would try to rescue her beloved mentor. They knew she'd be alone, too proud to ask for help. They believed, tripping on her own conceit, she would fail trying.

Karsh and Ileana would be out of the way.

Leaving them a clear path to capture the twins.

They knew Ileana would come, all right. The only question was "How soon?"

CHAPTER FOUR
THE SUBSTITUTE

"Can you believe Coach Mills just added another practice to the schedule? And that new rule? Miss a practice without a valid excuse and you're off the team? It's taking that zero-tolerance thing where it was never meant to go." Cam tried to come off offended about their school soccer team's tough new policy, but even to her own ears she sounded phony.

It was last-period social studies. The bell had rung a few minutes earlier, but their teacher was tardy, so the entire class of tenth graders was taking an extended gab op. Cam had flipped around to face Beth, who sat directly behind her. All day long she'd been trying to make up with her. All day long the frizzy-topped brunette had resisted, giving Cam the cold shoulder. No big. Cam firmly believed she was wearing her down.

A belief that was totally borne out when Beth slipped Cam a folded note. *Don't open it now*, she mouthed, indicating the others in the class.

Cam took the note and rattled on, "I guess Coach thinks we need it. We haven't exactly been racking up wins this year."

Brianna Waxman, petite and wired, was in the seat next to Beth. With a toss of her blond-on-blond high-lighted hair, she smoothly slipped into their convo. "Reality check: Maybe Coach is trying to prevent a rerun of last year's disaster."

Ouch. Leave it to Bree to point out AGAIN that Cam blew the championship for them last year. And leave it to Beth to *not* point it out. Cam stashed Beth's note inside a book in her backpack, to read later.

Beth turned on Bree. "For most of the season, the Marble Bay Meteorites ruled. Cam was the reason why. End of story."

As if Bree was letting Beth have the last word. With a shrug of her pointy shoulders, she added, "Don't take this the wrong way, but we could use another A-list player. What about Alex? Sure you can't get her to sign up?"

Cam shook her head. "Not gonna happen. My new-found clone prefers it alone. She's such not the joiner."

"Speaking of which," Beth noted, nodding toward the front of the classroom, "seems our regularly scheduled teacher has decided not to join us after all."

Bree looked up and chortled, "Substitute teacher alert!"

Before Cam could flip around to see the new teacher, she heard the substitute call out, "Settle down, people. Give me your attention!"

Cam felt her insides turn to jelly.

She didn't have to turn around, nor did she need Alex's hyperkeen hearing. Cam recognized that scratchy voice.

It couldn't be!

Cam twisted slowly in her seat. And locked eyes with the one person in the world she never expected to see again.

The *shoplifter*?!

Her hair was jet-black now and pulled back into a bun. But her eyes, the ones Cam had seen behind the sunglasses, dark and buglike, bored into Cam. Without seeming surprised, she explained to the class, "Your regular teacher, Ms. Jameson, was called away on a family emergency. It may take several weeks until she returns. I'm Cecilia Webb and for the foreseeable future, I'll be running this class."

Cam's breath caught in her throat. A zillion questions buzzed in her brain. But *she's a thief! She can't be a teacher . . . can she? I knew it! We should have reported her! Is she following me? And . . .* loudest of all: *Alex! Where are you now that I need you?*

Alex was not in this class. She had PE last period.

Cam didn't think she could make it through the forty-eight-minute period alone. Desperately, she tried to telepathically connect with Alex. But her twin was too far away. Neither had been able to do that from much of a distance. She had to get closer.

Her hand shot up.

Ms. Webb responded with a withering glance. "A question, Miss . . . what *is* your name?"

"May I . . . please be excused? I left something in my locker," Cam stuttered.

"I asked what your name is."

Flushed, she responded, "Camryn Barnes. Please. I . . . kind of . . . need a book for this class."

"Request denied." Then, in a tone that matched her withering stare, she added, "Camryn Barnes."

Beth let out a low whistle, shocked.

Taken aback, Bree whispered, "Harsh."

Cam had to deal. Alone.

Cecilia Webb took charge of the class swiftly. She

told them that she intended to pick up where Ms. Jameson left off, that she would not tolerate students who regarded substitutes as an excuse to slack off.

The world history unit they were on was "Presidents, Prime Ministers, and People in Power," and the slithery substitute delved into it, calling on kids at random to see if they were prepared. Cam actually was — but no one could have guessed it from her pfumpfering.

"What President was the first U.S. secretary of state?" That was Cam's question. She totally knew the answer was —? It would come to her. . . . It was . . . uh — no, not Madeleine Albright. Uh . . .

"Thomas Jefferson." Right, except it was Beth who said it. Ms. Webb frowned, so Beth hastily added, "Oh, was that one for Cam? I thought you were looking at me."

Cecilia Webb regarded Beth suspiciously. "Thank you, Miss —"

"Fish, Beth," she answered with a bright smile. "And, ooops, sorry. I'll be more careful to only answer the questions directed at me."

Bree whispered, "Suck up much?"

But Webb bought Beth's excuse. She smiled right back at the freckled student. "An understandable error. And the correct answer is always appreciated. Now, this one is for Miss Barnes."

Thankful for Beth's save, Cam responded, "George Bush — the first one," to the question, "What President was formerly U.S. ambassador to the U.N. and head of the CIA?"

Her "turn" over, Cam tuned out for the rest of the period. She and Alex had not told anyone, not Dave nor Emily nor her brother, Dylan, about thwarting the shoplifting. They hadn't even spoken about it themselves. Last night, they hadn't thought there was much else to say about it.

Wrong.

Could it just be some galactic coincidence that the woman they'd caught shoplifting now turned into a substitute teacher? She needed Alex.

Cam didn't see her sister for the next several hours. No fan of Marble Bay High, Alex usually bolted when the final bell rang. She'd probably be halfway home — or wherever Als might decide to detour — by the time Cam deposited her books in her locker.

And Cam could not dash home today. Soccer practice was directly after class. In spite of her screwup last year, Cam was still the team's best hope for a championship.

When the bell rang, Cam, Bree, and Beth were

nearly to the door, when Ms. Webb called out, "Miss Fish, may I have a word with you?" Her tone, for the first time that day, was open and friendly. She added, "Just for a moment. You'll catch right up with your friends."

Don't! Cam wanted to scream. She nearly grabbed Beth's elbow to stop her. But Beth had already said, "Go ahead, I'll meet you guys on the field."

Cam was hyperventilating. This was so about her! Webb was totally going to pump Beth for info about Cam. Webb would want to know if Cam recognized her. And how much Cam had told Beth about the shoplifting.

Practice did not go well. Correction: Cam did not play well. Instead of focusing on the plays, she kept checking her watch. Where *was* the girl? What was Webb asking Beth about Cam? How long was Webb going to hold her after class?

A half hour. Thirty-four minutes, to be exact. That's how late Beth was to practice, a fact that Coach insisted on noting — although staying late in class for a teacher conference was a valid excuse.

In the locker room after practice, Cam finally got a moment to talk to her friend alone. Trying to mask her anxiety, she said, "What the dilly-yo with the substitute? Don't tell me she gave you a hard time."

Beth scrunched her forehead. "No dilly-yo, really. She's just trying to get her bearings. It's kinda hard being dropped in to someone else's class three months into the semester."

"Did she say anything about me?" Cam asked nervously.

"No," Beth responded coolly.

"You were there for a long time with her."

Beth shrugged, annoyed now. "We got to talking. I guess I didn't notice the time."

"Talking — if not about any of the students, or the work, then what?"

"It was interesting. Ms. Webb was telling me how she loves teaching, what a wonderful feeling she gets helping kids realize their potential." Beth continued earnestly, "Then she mentioned she does a lot of volunteer work, because that also gives her a great sense of satisfaction."

I'll bet, Cam thought as an uneasy feeling washed over her.

Jittery, but trying to keep her voice light, Cam asked, "But you didn't, like, sign up for any volunteer thing with her, did you?"

"In fact, I did," Beth said.

CHAPTER FIVE
TUNING OUT

Alex was sitting cross-legged on the floor of Dylan's room next to him.

The volume on the amplifiers had been turned up to earsplitting. No wonder Dylan didn't hear Cam come blasting through the front door, shouting her twin's name. No normal person could. Alex could. *Her* decision to ignore Cam was deliberate.

Alex wasn't peeved at her sister. She just didn't want to tip Dyl off to her extraordinary aural ability. Though not a warlock, Dylan was no dummy: He'd deduce something was up. It was hard enough keeping their powers secret from the rest of the world — hiding them from the brother they lived with was a whole 'nother challenge. Besides, she was having fun. So no matter what her soccer-babe sis was bellowing about, Cam could wait.

Dylan was sharing something with her. The boy was all about music, and for the past several hours he'd been riffing joyously, courtesy of the brand-spanking-new electric guitar he'd received from Dave and Emily.

"Listen to this!" Dylan would go, over and over, eyes closed, as his nimble fingers flicked across the six-string, bending and moving the sound like an electric poet. And, "Oh, man, no wait — listen to this!"

"Sweet!" Alex would respond, over and over again as she sang along, and every once in a while, offered an original lyric.

If Dylan was all about playing, she was all about composing. Not that she'd ever had anything this expensive to compose on exactly. The cheesy third and fourth-hand excuse-for-guitars she'd had back in Montana could never come close to making any sounds like this.

Music was a secret Alex had kept from family Barnes. She hadn't told them what it meant to her, but somehow Dylan had sensed it.

What he couldn't know were the bittersweet memories it brought. Music would always remind Alex of her mom.

Sara.

It was one connection they could count on. When they had nothing, they still had music. Correction: Alex had a gift for it. And Sara had a gift for listening, singing along (tunelessly) with her daughter. To Alex, Sara's off-key vocals were the most beautiful she would ever hear. She would never be able to listen to the classic "Sara Smile" — their favorite — without bawling.

She'd not picked up a guitar, or even listened to much music, since Sara got sick. It had been a *long* time.

Except that now, as she and Dylan harmonized, Alex felt a glimmer, and she remembered: the rush of creating, of that magical moment when the sound was exactly right. There were times she felt her own veins and arteries to be guitar strings, as if the music played her.

Dylan was offering a tangible gift, too. His old guitar. Old! Only in this family would it be considered dispensable. It just so happened to be a Taylor acoustic, made of tiger maple wood. Alex knew it was costly, rare even.

No way could she take it! She'd been dead serious about not accepting gifts from clan Barnes, refusing Emily's offer of new clothes, Dave's for a personal laptop.

No way could she not! What was Dylan going to do with it anyway, she rationalized as her fingers lingered over the exquisite blond spruce face. It was probably just going to sit around, unused.

And it was being offered by a boy she really had no trouble thinking of as family. Strange.

Dylan was Emily and Dave's bio-baby; Cam had lived with him all her life, and it had been clear to Alex that Cam and Dylan shared a bond. In this equation, Alex would be one sister too many.

But a funny thing happened on the way to Barnes family dynamics class: Als had somehow bonded with Dylan. Cam was the one who sometimes felt pushed aside.

That feeling reared its envious head when Cam finally figured out where her sister was — she came barreling into the room, and, when her shouting and motioning didn't get Alex's attention, in one swift, impulsive motion, pulled the plug on the amplifier. The sudden silence shook the room.

"Whoa! What the . . . what'd you do that for?" Dylan jerked his head up.

Hands on her hips, Cam said churlishly, "I need to talk to Alex. She knows this. She totally heard me calling. Yet somehow, she chose to ignore me. This seemed like the best way of getting through to her."

At least I didn't blow up the amplifier, Cam said telepathically to Alex. *I could have made sparks fly, you know!* Cam's ability to set things on fire was her favorite guilty pleasure.

Douse the flames, firestarter-girl, Alex replied. *Whatever it is you've come to tell me probably isn't worth huffing and puffing and burning the house down.*

Dylan looked puzzled. "Dude, how could she know? Neither of us heard you. And all you had to do was turn the volume down, not stomp in here like some crazy banshee. Chill out!"

"Chill?" Cam gritted her teeth. If she were any colder, stalagmites and stalagtites would sprout from her ribs. "I don't exactly feel like chilling right now, bro. So you'll excuse me, Donny, if I borrow Marie for a while."

Alex was amused. Cam wasn't even trying to hide her jealousy. How totally un-Cami-like. The girl who always liked to be in control of her emotions was totally out of control now. Princess Camryn was so used to getting her way exactly when she wanted it, she went ballistic if she didn't get instant gratification.

Alex immediately felt bad about that thought. Clearly, Cami had something serious to spill. She stood up and handed Dylan the acoustic guitar. "Later, dude, we'll pick up where we left off."

Intending to scoot out of the room quickly and deal with Cam, something stopped Alex in her tracks just then. The faintest whiff of it caught in her nostrils, and her stomach turned. Someone had been smoking cigarettes in this room.

Cam closed the door of the bedroom the twins shared and began to rant, "I've been trying to tell you — shoplifter woman! Substitute teacher! Same person!"

Alex flounced on her bed. "So you're buggin' because we didn't report her?"

She was exactly that. She paced the room.

While Alex agreed the coincidence was beyond bizarre, she refused to travel down the road her twin was on.

Cam insisted they had to turn her in.

Alex insisted they couldn't. First of all, nothing was taken — *they* had returned the merchandise. What were they going to report to the cops — an attempted robbery? Like that would stick or even matter.

Cam absentmindedly twirled the chain of her sun necklace around her finger. "I can make her confess!"

"Really?" Alex drawled. "How?"

"I can, you know, stare at her — stun her!"

"Using your laser-beam eyes, you mean? Set her on fire? In front of the class? Or are you planning to do it onstage in the auditorium maybe? Oh, I know — you can do it at the school talent show! That'll be a winner!"

Alex's mocking, meant to show Cam she was overreacting, had the opposite effect. Cam grew more frustrated. "What part of this don't you get? Webb is the lowest of the low — a skanky thief who uses kids to do her dirty work. Who knows what else she's capable of?"

"Aren't you forgetting something?" Alex pointed out. "We have something on her — not vice versa. She should be freaking out. Maybe she's even quit by now. Webb doesn't know why we didn't turn her in. For all she knows, we will."

"If she was about to run," Cam reminded her, "she would have bolted out the door when the bell rang. Instead, she bonded with Beth. This slimeball is here to stay. And she's making my life miserable."

Alex sighed. "Then we wait."

"Until?"

"Until she screws up and gives us a reason to turn her in. Meantime, you'll keep an eye on her — no flamethrowers, just an eye. And I'll keep an ear . . ."

"We might not have a meantime," Cam retorted. "She's got Beth involved in some scheme."

"Scheme? You think Beth is gonna be stealing bracelets out of the Jewelry Corner? Paranoia is not your best accessory."

"I have to tell Beth not to listen to Webb, not to have anything to do with her." Cam grabbed the portable phone, about to hit speed-dial.

Alex closed her eyes and concentrated hard. She pictured the phone flying out of Cam's hands. Instantly, the receiver propelled itself five feet into the air — Alex took a step toward it and caught it.

"Why'd you do that?" Cam demanded.

"Because I would be remiss in my sisterly duties if I didn't say . . . *bad plan, Cam*! Your BFF is not going to be cool with your cease-and-desist bulletin."

"Point taken. Now give me back the phone before *I* do a little magic trick — promise, it'll be a sizzler!" She eyeballed the pink receiver threateningly.

"Don't bother. Here." Alex returned the phone to Cam. "You've been warned."

Nothing Alex said could have prepared Cam for Beth's reaction.

To Cam's urgent "Listen, I've gotta tell you something important," Beth quickly responded, "Cami? I'm really glad you called. I've got something . . . Did you read the note I passed you?"

"Note? What note?" Cam blurted. Then she remembered. Beth passed her a note in social studies, asking her to read it later. She'd forgotten all about it.

Beth let out a long sigh. "Okay, you didn't. But I've got to talk to you —"

Cam cut in. "Wait, this is totally urgent."

Beth pressed on, "No, you wait. So is this. Cam . . . are you alone? I mean, is Alex in the room? Can she hear us?"

"Yeah, but it's cool. Als knows why I'm calling."

Beth lowered her voice. "Listen, Cami. Could you call me back on the cell phone? When you're alone? There's something I . . ."

Exasperated, Cam blurted, "You can't do that volunteer thing with Webb."

Beth was taken aback. "What? What are you talking about? Why not?"

"You just have to believe me. Tell Webb you've changed your mind."

"Is this one of your mojo things?" Beth asked suspiciously.

"Yes. I mean, no. It's . . . it's just . . . you have to . . ." Cam stammered.

"You know what, Cam? Put the mojo on slow-mo for a moment and give me a reason. A real reason that makes sense to someone who isn't a twin and doesn't have hunches. A normal reason for a normal person. Like me."

Alex, who'd heard everything, snickered. *What are you going tell her? Or did you just think she'd do what you asked, no reason required?"*

Cam glared her at twin. Into the phone she said the first thing that popped into her head. "It's gonna take up too much time. You'll miss too many soccer practices."

"That's what you think is so important? I might miss soccer?"

"You could be booted off the team," Cam insisted stubbornly.

"Okay — now you listen," Beth said. "A) No I won't. And B) So what? What if I decide something else is more important than soccer?"

"I need you there." Cam knew she was being mulish. And pathetic.

Beth actually snickered. "Oh! So this is about you? Take a memo, Camryn. Everything isn't about you. Not always."

Cam stared at the phone, which had gone dead.

Confused and hurt, she sniped at Alex. "If I even hear the *first* words of you thinking 'I told you so,' you are toast. Burnt!"

Alex left the room.

Still clutching the phone, Cam sat on the bed, trying to think. She closed her eyes. A picture formed: a wise and weathered old man with nappy white hair and a sad smile. "I'll be here when you need me," he'd told her.

And then another, a striking blond woman with metallic-gray eyes, identical to hers and Alex's, snapping, "Call me Goddess."

Karsh and Ileana. The tracker and the vain but

valiant witch sworn to guide and protect the twins. To be there in times of danger.

Neither twin had seen or heard from their protectors in several weeks. What did that mean? They only came when Thantos was nearby — not when danger took the form of a spidery shoplifter? Or maybe there was no real danger.

If that were true, why did every bone in her body tell her otherwise?

CHAPTER SIX
FITTING IN

Dinner had become this big-deal thing. Check that, Alex thought. Emily's big-deal thing.

"Dinnertime is family time," Cam and Dylan's petite — and to Alex, unnaturally chirpy — mom insisted. Everyone had to eat together, at the same time every night. No TV allowed, no reading at the table, and totally no answering the phone. Regimented much?

Worse, this was all new. Things had been more casual before Alex arrived, just the foursome doing the chat 'n' chew thing around the kitchen table. Now they ate in the formal dining room, sitting stiffly on high-back upholstered chairs that matched the drapes, at a table way too huge for them.

"Since we've become five," Emily had said cheerfully, but often enough to rub in Alex's fifth-wheel status, "we don't fit in the kitchen anymore."

"Why don't you just say what you really mean?" Alex had challenged belligerently, a few weeks after she'd gotten there, leaning into Emily's shocked face. "That *I* don't fit!"

Emily had blinked back tears, which just proved Alex was right. The woman could pretend all she wanted, but at the core of it, Emily didn't want her here. Alexandra Fielding had totally messed up the symmetry of their lives.

Okay, so a part of Alex knew she was being unfair — she could hear Sara chiding her gently, "Give her time, baby, this isn't easy for her." But the others had made room for her quickly, in their lives and sort of in their hearts. So what was Emily's problem? Another part of Alex so didn't care. She'd had a mother who raised her, and another who bore her: Emily Barnes didn't fit into any emotional equation in her life.

This evening promised its own special brand of tense, since she and Cam were at odds. Alex stubbornly refused to be bent out of shape just because Cam's substitute teacher happened to be a shoplifter.

Cam needed to chill and see how things played out.

"So," Emily announced, swiping away too-long

bangs from her forehead, "tonight's experiment is . . ." She paused in this faux-dramatic way. "Chicken Kiev."

"Exactly what I was in the mood for!" Dave said, winking at Cam.

Part of Emily's new regime was her insistence on making dinner herself, and making it complicated. What was she thinking? Alex thought. If she morphed into Martha Stewart, everything would go back to the way it was? Under her control?

Only Emily Barnes didn't really have the time, talent, or inclination to be a doyenne of domesticity. And it showed.

Now she hovered over the table, looking hopeful, and dramatically lifted the lid off the ceramic baking dish. Cam smiled encouragingly. "You made this last week, Mom. It was . . . uh . . . really good."

"Only," Emily admitted, "I was rushing this morning, and I might not have defrosted it enough, so it might be a little rarer tonight."

Cam's curly-haired dad tried for a joke. "So what's a little salmonella among friends? I'm sure it's great." He grabbed his knife and sliced into the top piece. It was bright pink in the middle.

"I think I speak for the chicken when I say . . ." Dylan paused for effect, then yelled, "Ouch!"

Emily was not amused, especially as her son added,

"Yo, Moms, there's a difference between rare and alive." Then, he started flapping his elbows, doing a cheesed-out rendition of the funky chicken.

Alex burst out laughing. Not at Dylan's lame-o joke, but because she'd heard Cam think, *This could be a good time to announce that I'm going vegan.*

Emily thought Alex was mocking her. "I'd really appreciate you not encouraging him," she said in a clipped tone. "I'm doing my best."

Dave tried to squash his own amusement. "If it's too rare for you, Dylan, just take it into the kitchen and nuke it." With that, he helped himself to chicken, salad, green beans, and a baked potato.

"So, how was school today?" Emily's line, Alex thought, but delivered by Dave. The man was determined to be supportive of his wife's insistence on dinner chat.

When a mumbled chorus of "fines" greeted him, Dave chuckled, "Okay, I withdraw the question, on the grounds of 'too vague.'" He turned to Cam. "How'd soccer practice go?"

"Not that great," Cam admitted between forkfuls of salad — hoping her mom wouldn't notice her avoiding the chicken. "I wasn't real focused."

Emily looked up, concerned. "Is anything wrong?"

Only everything. Cam sighed. But full disclosure between her and Emily was a casualty of Alex's arrival, as was finding out that Dave knew more than his wife ever would about the twins. Well, maybe she could tell her mom some of it. "We have a substitute for social studies."

Emily's eyebrows arched. "And you don't like her? That's what interfered with your concentration in soccer?"

Without meaning to, Cam let her eyes drift to Alex. A gesture Emily caught. Before she could misinterpret and accuse *her* of throwing off Cam's game, Alex blurted, "Beth was a no-show at practice. Cam thinks she's mad at her."

Cam glared at Alex. *I so need you explaining things for me! You weren't even there!* Testily, Cam contradicted, "Beth got there late, and I do not think she's mad at me."

Touchy, touchy, twin-shine. I was just trying to help you back out of the corner you almost pushed yourself into. Or were you planning to connect Ms. Webb with soccer practice?

I don't need your —

Emily turned to Alex. "You know, I've been thinking. Soccer is such a great sport, and since you and Cam are so similar physically, I bet you'd be good at it. Why don't you try out for the team? It's not too late."

Hoping Emily noticed *she* was halfway through her chicken, Alex said casually, "Soccer's not my game."

"Is there any sport you do play?" Emily probed.

Yeah, Alex thought but didn't say. Where I grew up, we were all into croquet. And crew. Let's not forget tennis, with my titanium racquet.

Cam broke in, *Stop it!*

She can't hear me, Alex responded, running a hand through her streaked and choppy 'do. Out loud, she responded, "I'm not big on team sports."

Emily pressed on. "Something else, then? The yearbook, the literary magazine, photography, debate club? Any extracurricular activities will look good on your college application."

"Who said I'm going to college?"

Emily's jaw tightened, but before she could respond, Dave switched gears. "Guess what, Alex? The paperwork for us becoming your legal guardians is pretty much finished."

Alex tensed. She was not up for adoption. No way would she go that route. But she was underage and needed legal guardians. Alex had little choice but to go along with it. She could, and did, choose not to discuss it.

Tentatively, Emily asked, "So what's the next step?"

"We go through a standard evaluation process. A social worker will check us out, be sure we're suitable parents, that kind of thing."

Dylan elbowed Alex. "Oooh, this is like you'll be our

foster child. Maybe we'll call you Little Orphan Alex. Or Harry Potter. We could build you a cupboard under the stairs. . . ."

Cam cracked up and was relieved to see a slow grin forming on her twin's face. Alex elbowed Dyl. "Oh, yeah? If I'm Harry Potter, that makes you fat cousin Dudley. I think I'll call you that from now on."

"You do and I'll take back that guitar I gave you," he joked, turning excitedly to his parents. "You should hear us riff together. We rocked the house this afternoon!"

Emily frowned. "This afternoon? Didn't you have basketball practice today?"

Dylan took his time before responding, chewing deliberately. "Oh, yeah, I meant to tell you. I'm off the team."

"What?" Emily looked horrified.

"Whoa, Moms, chill. It's not like I said I *offed* someone, I'm just off the team."

That drew Dave's wrath. "Don't speak to your mother like that."

Emily tried to censor herself but couldn't, and went with her first instinct. "You didn't get kicked off? I mean, we would have heard . . ."

Alex tensed for the wave of Emily's blame surely coming her way.

Dylan shrugged. "I didn't get kicked off. I quit."

It was Dave's turn to be taken aback. "Why? And why didn't you tell us?"

"There wasn't anything to tell. Basketball's not my thing anymore."

"Your *thing*?" Emily's voice went up an octave. "What *is* your thing, then?"

"I don't know. Music maybe," Dylan said defensively. "Do I have to decide my whole life right now?"

If Emily was trying to keep herself from shooting Alex a glare, she didn't succeed.

"If you're thinking I had anything to do with this —" Alex started, but Emily cut her off.

"You have no idea what I'm thinking," Emily inserted. "You may be very talented, Alex, but I doubt you can read minds."

Cam braced for the thought Alex was about to shoot her way. . . .

Can't I, Auntie Em? Just shows what you know.

. . . And hurled a retort at her twin. *Shut up!*

Dave leveled a glance at his son. "Well, I'm really disappointed that you made this decision without even telling us. It's not like you."

Cam's double-earringed bro tipped his chair backward. "You're all making a big deal about nothing. So I'm not on the team. So what?"

Dave, in peacemaker mode, quickly interjected, "You know what? We'll talk about this later. Clear the table, deal with the dishes, all three of you."

The phone rang and Emily, ignoring her own rule, sprang up to get it. Dave announced, "I'm going into the den; I've got some work to catch up on. Not that anybody asked, but my day wasn't so great, either."

Alex's face fell. He'd worked on the guardianship papers all day, and now she was giving Emily a hard time. Is that what had gotten him down?

Sensing her discomfort, Dave explained, "It's nothing to do with you, Alex. A new case is frustrating."

"The same one you had to go into the office for on Sunday?" Cam asked.

He nodded. "There's been a rash of shoplifting episodes, mostly by kids. It's looking like a pattern."

Together, Cam and Alex said, "Shopliftings?"

Dave explained, "Run like a sting operation. A twosome, usually an older woman and a younger girl, enter a jewelry store. They ask to see an expensive piece of jewelry. The older woman then distracts the salesperson . . ."

"While the teenager replaces the piece with a fake?" Cam finished, her stomach slowly sinking.

"How'd you . . . guess?" Dave started to ask, but

stopped. He knew something about Cam's premonitions, or "hunches." "Anyway," he continued, "in the last heist, the kid got caught and I'm representing her."

"What about the woman with her, does she have another attorney?" Cam asked, but she already knew the answer. Which was: "She got away."

"And the girl refuses to identify her accomplice?" Alex guessed.

"Right again."

"Dad?" Cam paused. "Can you tell us your client's name?"

CHAPTER SEVEN
BETH'S FROST

Cam was on high alert. She couldn't squash the feeling — stronger than ever now — that Webb needed to be brought to justice. That she needed to get Webb off her back — and away from Beth.

Alex had no such feeling. Correction: Als insisted they had to play it cool. Wait until Webb tripped up. Until then, keep a close eye on Beth.

That wasn't good enough for Cam, who kept Alex up half the night, pacing and fretting. The usually rational twin kept insisting they had to tell Dave about the shoplifting they'd intercepted. Which forced Alex to play her "bad plan" tape again. While Dave knew about the twins' heritage, she reminded Cam, he didn't know about their powers. "The less he knows, the safer he is. If Karsh wanted him to know, he would have told him."

There it was again. Karsh. The information the weathered, wise old warlock had — and had not — given them. It was beginning to overshadow everything else in their lives. Cam had a burning need to step out of those shadows into the bright, if sometimes brutal, truth of sunlight, which conflicted with Alex's instinct to let the shadows linger awhile, until she found her own way.

"Als," Cam had said finally, on the verge of giving up, "at the very least, wear your necklace, OK? I'll feel more secure. Humor me."

Karsh had given Alex a necklace, a half-moon charm that he later explained had been crafted by her biological father, Aron. It fit perfectly into Cam's half-sun necklace, forming a circle.

The very first time the twins had worn them together, something magical had happened. As if super-magnetized, the sun and moon had pulled toward each other, desperate to fit together!

And when they did, the sisters heard a voice. . . . A faint yet sure, faraway voice, a man. Followed by another, dulcet and loving. Could it have been Miranda and Aron? The twins had no way of knowing . . . yet.

*   *   *

"Cam! Alex!" Dave called as they pulled up to school the next morning. "Rise and shine! Cute as the two of you look dozing in the backseat, the slumber-number gig is up. We're almost there."

Blearily, Cam lifted her head from Alex's shoulder, where it had apparently drooped when they'd dozed on the short ride to school. She yawned and fumbled for her backpack. "*Gracias* for the lift, padre. We totally wouldn't have made it if we'd had to walk." Cam leaned over and gave Dave a peck on the cheek.

Alex rubbed her eyes, clearing the cobwebs from her brain. "We wouldn't want to chance a tardy tarnishing Cami's perfect attendance record."

Cam shook her head. "Speaking of tarnishing, your eyeliner's trashed. Free beauty tip of the day: Rub eyes equals smush makeup."

Alex grinned. "*Merci*, Bobbi Brown. That's the look I was going for. Smush-goth."

At least, Cam thought, alighting from the car, Alex was wearing her necklace. Cam wasn't entirely sure what power the amulets held, only that they were stronger when the girls wore them together.

Too bad she had no power to warm up the chill wind that her best bud had become in her presence.

In the morning classes they shared, Beth barely

spoke to her. Which was in vivid contrast to the complete Oprah she'd become to everyone else. In science, she shared an in-joke ("Okay, so this amoeba slithers into a bar . . .") with brainiac mate Sukari, leaving Cam out. In Spanish, she traded notes with Six Packer Kristen Hsu. During math class, Cam heard her whispering to Bree. In PE, she passed the volleyball to everyone on her side — except Cam.

In English lit, Cam sent her an "I'm sorry" note, but Beth made a point of not reading it. With a pang Cam realized she still hadn't read Beth's. She scrambled to find it, but she got called on just then.

There was no thaw at lunch. Cam had gotten to the cafeteria a little late. She'd stopped to try and convince Alex to A) fix her makeup ("You've made your subversive point"); and B) come eat with the Six Pack ("Everyone wants you to join us"). She'd failed on both counts. Ornery Als insisted on keeping her goth look and brown-bagging it outdoors with Dylan's ragtag bunch rather than be "another stripe in your Rainbow Brite Gang."

So by the time Cam arrived, most of her friends were already eating. Beth was seated — on purpose? — between carrottopped Amanda Carter and Brianna. Cam sat across from them, next to Kristen. She was determined to try and talk to Beth, only her BFF launched into an animated convo with Amanda.

"We can all sign up," Beth said, taking a huge bite of her tuna sandwich. "It's the one Ms. Webb works for. She's going to bring some more info for me after class today."

"Sign up for what?" Bree asked between mini bites of salad and a diet cola.

"Helping Hands," Amanda responded. "Beth's been telling me about it. It's this group that runs a shelter for abused and abandoned kids."

Helping Hands? *That's* what Beth had joined? That charity thing from the mall? With that cute guy, Shane? How tangled *was* this Webb? Cam lost her appetite.

In one smooth motion, Sukari slid onto the bench and into the chat. "So what all would you do? Baby-sit the kids? Read to them or something?"

"Uh-uh." Beth shook her head and wiped a bit of mayo from the corner of her mouth. "They have a paid staff for that. Our job is to raise money to keep the place running. Wait, they have a mission statement." From her backpack, she withdrew a pamphlet — the same one from the cart at the mall, Cam noticed — and read, "'Because we believe that every child is entitled to a safe, secure, and stable environment, Helping Hands is dedicated to improving the quality of life for at-risk children. To make a positive difference in the life of even one child is to be truly blessed.'" She passed the brochure to

Amanda and Bree. Photographs of sad-looking children clutching stuffed animals stared out at them.

Amanda spontaneously teared up. "These poor babies. I'm signing up."

Sukari reached over the table to scan the pamphlet. Warily, she asked, "How do they expect you to raise money?"

"That's what this afternoon's meeting is about," Beth explained. "Ms. Webb is going to explain the process."

Cam couldn't restrain herself. "Just make sure the process isn't . . ." *Illegal* was the word she wanted to scream, but "anything too intense" is what she settled for.

Deep brown eyes flashing, Beth turned on Cam. "What *is* your problem with this? Forget it, don't answer. We know Cam isn't joining." Beth's frostiness took everyone by surprise.

"Why not? You're all about little kids, Cam," Sukari asked.

"Because her mojo told her it's a no-go," Beth muttered.

Cam wanted to explain, but she caught something out of the corner of her eye. A teacher entered the cafeteria from the side door. A teacher wearing a long black duster over matching slacks and dark spike-heeled boots. Webb.

Cam felt her skin prickle and her stomach tighten.

She eyed Webb again. The shifty substitute was striding across the room, in the direction of Principal Hammond, who was patrolling the cafeteria.

"What about you, Bree?" Beth was now teasing. "Beneath that superficial yet highly exfoliated skin surely beats the heart of a closet humanitarian. Join with?"

Bree scrunched her pert, upturned nose. "So you don't actually have to be around the kids? Play with them or anything? That could be" — she fished for the word — "messy."

Beth laughed. "Relax, it's about keeping the shelter up and running."

"Fine. Just tell me where to donate." Bree reached for her wallet.

"Come on, you guys, it's about saving little children. Where are your hearts?" Amanda, who wore hers on her sleeve, demanded.

Kristen shook her head. "Tempted as I am, time's at a premium. Bree and I signed up for the dance committee this morning. We're doing decorations. Between that and soccer there's no way."

The winter dance was two weeks away. Sponsored by the parent-teacher organization and held in the gym, it was the school's first big social event of the season. This year's theme was Winter Wonderland.

"So we have to transform the gym into a fiesta-worthy environment," Kris was explaining. "Challenging much?"

"Speaking of," Bree said, turning to Kris, "how'd you respond to the challenge issued by Craig? Are you going with him?"

Kris nodded. "I am. What about you? Decide yet?"

"It's between Jon, Tanner, and this tempting new junior, Marco." Bree explained of the last one, "He's in the drama club, supposed to be a really good actor."

Sukari's friend-protecting radar went up. "Watch it, Ms. Brianna — just be sure he's not playin' you because of your dad."

Bree's father was a big-time Hollywood producer. A fact she made sure the entire school knew. What no one knew, except for Bree's closest friends, was that since her parents' divorce ten years ago, she had little contact with him. Now she sniffed her "like I couldn't tell?!" sniff and changed the subject. "You're going, right, Beth? I mean, getting in touch with your inner humanitarian doesn't cancel out having fun. You know what they say, 'All activism and no play . . .'"

"I am totally going to the dance. Not," she sighed overdramatically, "that I have a date, but. . . ."

"Don't need one," Sukari cut in cheerfully. "It's not a mating dance — lots of people are going solo. Better chance of meeting someone that way."

The tap on her shoulder was a light one, but Cam jumped as if someone had come up behind her and gripped her hard. She flipped around, fully expecting the evil eye of Webb. Or worse.

So there was no way Jason Weissman, the lanky senior who was into her, could have interpreted her expression: a morph from panic to relief in a micro-second. He smiled sheepishly. "Sorry, I didn't mean to freak you out."

Cam heard her friends snickering as she stammered, "You d-didn't. I mean, you did . . . but . . ."

"So, anyway, uh, can I talk to you for a minute?" Jason shifted his weight from one foot to the other and eyed her hopefully.

"Sure." Cam shot her buds a "cut it out" look and followed the buff boy across the room.

Cam totally liked him. Athletic, smart, and hot, still Jason was not a show-off or a player. He was a nice guy — and okay about being a nice guy. Only, she wasn't sure if she liked him because of all his worthy qualities, or if she *liked* liked him.

Jason found a spot by the vending machine and stopped. He self-consciously shoved his hands in his jeans pockets. "So what's up? Why are you so jumpy? Not that you have to tell me."

Suddenly shy — how unlike her! — Cam focused

on the floor. "I'm just stressin' about social studies," she found herself telling him.

"You? Go-to-the-head-of-the-class Cam? Hey, if you need tutoring . . ."

"It's not the work. Yesterday, we got this evil demon substitute teacher."

"Well, the good thing about evil demon substitutes is that they *leave.*"

"Not this one. She's gonna be a fixture for a while. Anyway." Cam gazed up into Jason's big dark brown eyes. "I have a hunch that's not what you wanted to talk about."

"You and your hunches. Right again. It's about the dance. You going?"

Cam decided to make it easy on him. "Are you asking me? 'Cause if you are, the answer's yes."

Relief flooded Jason's angular face. "Excellent! Then, I'll see you, I mean I'll pick you up . . . What am I saying? Of course I'll see you before then!"

Cam giggled. "Of course. Later." When she strode back to her friends, she couldn't hide the silly smile plastered across her face.

Which sent Bree's radar into hyperdrive. "Bet I know what's got our Cami all aglow — alpha girl strikes again, asked to the dance by the senior of her dreams."

Blushing, Cam protested, "He is so not! We're friends. He's a cool . . ."

But all five of her buds — Beth included, she noted happily — razzed her good-naturedly for the rest of the period. As they did, her protests became weaker. Because for a moment, Cam remembered what her life was like before Alex came into the picture. Before everything changed. Even if *she* never felt completely normal, her life, at least, was.

Those good feelings almost made her forget about the last period of the day.

CHAPTER EIGHT
BLINDED BY THE LIGHT

"Ms. Barnes" — Webb fixed a cold eye on her — "perhaps you can enlighten us. To which world leader is this historic quote attributed, and at what occasion did he — or she — say it: 'Let us never negotiate out of fear, but let us never fear to negotiate'?"

Nervously, Cam flipped through her textbook. Was that in last night's reading assignment? She thought she'd been prepared. But the total tarantula who stood at Ms. Jameson's desk was on a mission to prove otherwise.

Webb's way, the class quickly found out, was to unnerve them by lobbing rapid-fire questions at them. Ignoring volunteers, she chose victims randomly as if her goal was not education, but humiliation.

Still, Brianna deftly held her own, and Beth rarely missed a question. Of course *they* didn't get the really hard ones. And when they did, they got hints. Webb had phrased this question purposely so Cam wouldn't know if it was a U.S. President, a prime minister, or another world leader, male or female. Could Webb be more obvious? Marking down every wrong or "incomplete" answer, spider-woman was deliberately trying to take Cam's grades down a notch. Or several.

Messing with Cam's grades was a total hot button. She was beyond boiling. As Alex had pointed out, this slimeball should have been worried about Cam exposing her. So why was she baiting Cam instead? She obviously needed a little reminder. "Before I answer that, I have a question for you, Ms. Webb. It's sort of off topic, but it's really important."

"Go ahead." Ms. Webb tapped talon-shaped fingernails on the desk.

"I'd like to know your feeling about the means justifying the ends. Like, say, raising money for a righteous cause — would you stoop to doing something illegal, like shoplifting?"

Although Cam couldn't see Beth, who sat behind her, she knew her friend's eyes had just popped open wide. The whole class was staring at her.

The black-clad teacher paused, then shot Cam a

withering stare. "Now what makes you ask that, Ms. Barnes? Trying to distract me from making you answer a question you clearly don't know?" The class giggled. They thought Webb had one-upped her.

Cam answered evenly, "No, just wondering." Touché!

If Cam thought that would intimidate the teacher, make her rethink the victimizing, she was beyond wrong. Webb continued, "Well, Ms. Barnes, while that was a fascinating interlude, we're still waiting for an answer."

Brianna slid her platform-sandaled toe across the aisle that separated their desks, nudged Cam's ankle, a hint that she knew the answer. Cam made the mistake of glancing over at her friend.

"We're not tag-teaming here," Webb snarled. "Either you know the answer or you don't. Which is it, Ms. Barnes?"

She tried to conjure up the answer. Franklin Roosevelt? Napoleon? Golda Meir? Could have been any of those.

An unlikely source tried to break the tension. Scott Marino, freckle-faced class clown, blurted out, "She can't phone a friend?"

"Nor can she poll the audience," Ms. Webb rejoined without missing a beat, nor with a hint of humor. "This isn't a quiz show, Mr. Marino."

The distraction worked to Cam's advantage. An image of John F. Kennedy came to her. She nailed it.

Which didn't satisfy Ms. Webb, who sneered, "Incomplete. When did he say that? If you fail to answer both parts of the question, you get fifty percent — half credit."

Cam was fuming. No one else got two-part questions! Everyone else got hints! And she'd given the correct answer!

Webb was so asking for it. Did she need a reminder of what Cam could do? She's goin' down!

"Ms. Barnes, we still await your answer. You have five seconds."

Cam snapped. *You want an answer? How 'bout this?*

Cam telescoped in on Webb's bulging bug eyes. She'd done this before. During a soccer game last summer, she'd wished her opponent would trip, and unwittingly made it happen. Now her wits were totally about her. She recalled the words that had come to her that day and instantly revised them. *Treacherous teacher, you will not win. Blunder, and stumble, let the fun begin!*

Fun, however, was not in the cards. In a bad-timing moment of epic proportions, Scott Marino popped out of his seat — right into the path of Cam's penetrating stare.

Disoriented, he toppled over and shrieked, "I'm blind! Ahhh!! I can't see! Help!!"

Cam was mortified. She leaped out of her seat and ran over to him. "It's okay, you'll be okay in a sec," she whispered. "It's only temporary." She put her arm around him, attempting to help him up.

But Webb roughly edged her out of the way. "Scott? What happened? What's going on?"

He wailed, "I fell. Everything's too bright! The whole room's white! I can't see!"

Cam inserted herself between the teacher and the boy. She instructed, "Keep your eyes closed for a sec, blink. It'll be okay in a minute."

Ignoring her, Webb propelled him out the door, heading for the school nurse. But not before Cam heard Scott murmur, "Wait, stop. I think it's better. . . . I can see now. I'm okay."

Cam wasn't. Bummed and shaken, her eyes stinging, she dashed out the door. She had to find Alex. But she hadn't gotten two steps when Brianna grabbed her elbow and commanded, "Girls' room, stat!"

"What exactly just happened in there?" Bree demanded as soon as they were inside and had made sure they were alone.

"Scott had a weird hysterical blindness thing . . . ?" Cam replied weakly.

Bree's expertly shaped eyebrows arched. "Must be catching. Didn't the same thing happen to Lindsay on the soccer field?"

Great, not only had an innocent kid gotten the scare of his life, but Bree was suspicious. She was 0–2.

Cam fidgeted with her sun necklace. "Webb's an equal-opportunity agitator. She could give anyone a panic attack."

Bree pursed her lips. "Speaking of the wicked witch of Marble Bay High, are you, like, trying to get her to fail you?"

"Why do you say that?"

Brianna leaned into Cam. "Fact: Cruella de Vil was totally picking on you. But that bizarro question about shoplifting? What was up with that?"

"Look, I just . . . know something bad about her. She's not what she seems."

"Really?" Bree went on instant dirt alert. "Dish, now!"

Cam averted Brianna's "you've gotta tell me" stare and sent a silent message to her twin. *Alex, where are you?*

Right here, sis. Coming in the door.

Had she really heard that? Was Als near enough?

The girls' room door opened and Alex, beat-up messenger bag slung crosswise over her shoulder, sauntered in, eye makeup still defiantly smudged.

Brianna cracked, "Love the spin-art approach to makeup, Dyslexia. You've really got that evil twin thing nailed. But maybe you can figure out why your sister is trying to fail social studies. As for moi, I decorate, therefore, I bounce." Bree shouldered her Prada bag and headed out.

Alex took one look at her totally bummed-out sister and suggested, "To quote the local parlance — we should 'bounce,' too. A quiet place is . . . ?"

"Soccer field," Cam responded glumly. "No practice today."

A few minutes later, the twins settled on the empty bleachers overlooking the deserted field.

"So what are you doing here anyway?" Cam asked. "No jamming with Dylan today?"

"I heard you," Alex said gently, ignoring Cam's sarcasm. "You needed me."

"More than 'wishes he were Bob' Dylan?" Cam knew she was sounding whiny — jealous even — but was too tired to care.

Alex sighed. "Dudley Do-wrong has his own issues. I'll deal with him later. Cam, what's going on? What was Bree babbling about? What'd you do?"

Cam downloaded her twin on the whole bizarre social studies period, ending with her failure at tripping up Webb, and accidentally stun-gunning Scott Marino.

Alex was astonished. "You used your powers just because you might get what, a B? Dude, you're making progress!"

Cam grimaced. Alex thought it was funny when it had been a really stupid move. She'd reacted out of anger, without considering the consequences. That was the real bad plan. Something, some*one* —

Right. Karsh should have come and put a stop to it. Alex completed her thought.

"Als? Don't you think it's weird that we haven't seen or even heard from them in so long? Unless," Cam paused. "Unless you heard something and didn't tell me?"

"Not guilty," Alex responded. "Maybe this whole Webb deal isn't on their danger radar. Though you'd think 'gross misuse of powers' would be reason enough for Karsh. As for her, Little Miss 'Call Me Goddess' always seems like she's doing us the biggest favor by showing up."

"What if we try to call them?" Cam suggested.

"What? Just yell out?" Alex kidded. "It's not like we have the code, area or zip."

Cam twisted her hair into a ponytail and tied a scrunchie around it. "We could try an incantation."

"We don't know any that work for summoning," Alex reminded her.

"We've made up others on the spot," Cam countered. "We've got our necklaces."

Alex flipped her messenger bag open and pulled out paper at the exact same moment Cam got a pen out of her backpack.

Fifteen minutes later, Alex took Cam's hand. Their words floated over the empty soccer field.

Tracker and guardian, sworn to protect,
This dusky twilight, please come and connect.
We see danger approaching, evil encroaching.
Be there for us so we may unite,
To banish corruption, join together, and fight.

CHAPTER NINE
A TALE OF THREE BROTHERS

We see danger approaching, evil encroaching . . ."
Silently, Karsh finished the incantation. He could hear
the twins summoning him. It broke his heart that he
couldn't respond. He had promised to always be there
for them. A promise he never expected to break. But he
also hadn't expected to find himself in his current situation, hands bound by thick hemp cord that cut into his
wrists, legs chained at the ankles so he could not rise
without help. He could recite a spell and free himself,
but his captors would no doubt turn him into some easily squashable creature, like a caterpillar or slug. There
were two of them, both younger, stronger, and possibly

more powerful — and only one of him. They could, and would, overpower him in a split second.

Be there for us so we may unite,
To banish corruption, join together, and fight.

Karsh wanted desperately to respond telepathically, allow the twins to hear his calming voice in their heads. Camryn believed they were in danger; now Alexandra seemed to agree. By the words of their incantation he knew Ileana had not come to their aid, either. That distressed him more than anything. It meant his impetuous young charge was falling into the very trap set for her — that she would try to rescue him, instead of them. If he could accomplish only one thing in his disabled state, he would warn Ileana.

He heard the dangerously creaking, wooden steps groaning under the weight of heavy boots, followed by a lighter, but not more deft step. Quickly, Karsh dashed his own thoughts. His captors were also masterful mind readers.

"Very shrewd, you wily fox, scramble your thoughts as a radio dial caught between stations. An old trick." Thantos now towered over Karsh, menacing and mean, stroking his full black beard. "Fitting for an *old* man."

The most ruthless and powerful of warlocks had held Karsh captive here in this mildewed basement for nearly two weeks. Not that he'd personally carried out the abduction or even planned it, for that matter. This turn of events had been made possible by Fredo, the other warlock, who'd backed into it, really, and now sat sulking in a corner of the room.

"Why don't we just get rid of him?" the reedy-voiced Fredo whined. "I'll do it!"

Thantos swiftly whirled around and pointed at Fredo. "You will do exactly as I command you. What I say and when I say so. Until then, keep your ideas in a place where I can't even hear them."

"You never think any of my ideas are good!" Fredo pouted and crossed his bony arms sullenly.

"When you finally have one, I'll let you know!" Thantos thundered back at him, and Fredo cowered into his corner.

In spite of his situation, Karsh couldn't help being amused. Their behavior now was not unlike what it had always been, when the brothers were children.

Thantos, the eldest, had been a large boy. Now, at six foot five inches tall, dark and muscular, he'd grown into an imposing man. He'd always had a mean streak — as a kid, he was a bully. As a man, he'd become a brute, ruthlessly driving the family business, CompUmag, into one of the richest and most powerful conglomerates in the world. Lord Thantos — or Mr. Sot Naht, as he was known in the outside world — was "the brawn," and he wielded immense and terrifying power.

Fredo, the youngest, had been a slight and sickly kid. None too bright, it had taken him three years, instead of the customary six months, to pass Coventry Island's initiation tests and attain the rank of full-fledged warlock. He still was not an able tracker, and although he had learned the skill of transmutation, there were few forms he could really take. A huge and monstrous lizard was his favorite.

Fredo had grown older, but had never grown up. Now he'd become a dangerously inept adult, always trying to curry favor with his big brother. Until recently, Thantos had been content to allow Fredo to do some of his bidding. It kept the simpleton out of his way, and more important, away from CompUmag. Fredo was, and remained, the baby of the family.

In between those extremes was Aron, the middle brother. A handsome and exceptionally brilliant boy, he was first in his class in all subjects. Aron rose through the ranks of warlocks from guardian to tracker, shape-shifter, master of transmutation, and on to mentor. He'd been the youngest ever in all of Coventry Island's history to be awarded a lordship.

Yet Aron had refused to "lord" his gifts over anyone.

He believed those who stood tallest were those who stooped to help others. All on Coventry Island accepted their destiny to serve humankind; Aron believed that in his heart.

It was Aron who'd started the company, Comp-Umag; it was Aron's dream to develop and use technology for the good of all. More than a visionary, Aron was the brother smart enough to turn his dreams and ideas into reality.

Aron had been the brightest of the brothers.

Fredo had never grasped that simple fact.

Because Thantos did, he was wildly jealous. He coveted everything Aron had.

He still did.

"Camryn and Alexandra are my nieces, my blood. They will come to me, and there is nothing you can do to stop that!" Thantos had ranted at Karsh repeatedly for the past two weeks.

"And you believe that by keeping me from them —" Raising his sparse, wispy eyebrows just slightly, Karsh had continued wearily, "that they will fall into your clutches, just like that? You give me too much credit, Lord Thantos."

Thantos's mouth twisted into an evil grin. "I am not crediting you, doddering fool. You know why I have you here."

"You're the bait!" Fredo crowed, feeling brave enough now to rise from his corner of the room and head over toward Karsh.

"Shut up, you imbecile!" Thantos roared, stopping Fredo in his tracks.

"All we want," Thantos had told Karsh threateningly on that first day, "is a little bit of your time. Not that, by the looks of it, you have that much left!"

Silently, Karsh cursed the infirmities of his advanced age. A younger man would not be bowed by arthritis, by weakened bones; a healthier specimen would not need to rely on the elixirs and potions to keep the constant pain at bay.

His younger, stronger self would not have been hoodwinked by Thantos, or kidnapped by Fredo in the first place.

It happened the very night Ileana had brought Fredo back from Marble Bay, to the steps of the Coventry Island Unity Council. Yes, Lady Rhianna was there, ready to take him into custody, but the Exalted Elder on her own could not stop Fredo from shape-shifting into a giant lizard. Ileana had not bothered to follow the rules, to be sure there were three Elders in attendance when she brought him in. Startled by his rank insubordination, Lady Rhianna had not reacted quickly enough. Fredo had gotten away.

His destination was not Thantos's mansion on the mainland. Too terrified of his brother's wrath to show up empty-handed, he'd hatched a plan to capture Karsh. Fredo wasn't as smart as the wise Karsh, but he could, and did, use the shock of surprise.

A stealth attack.

Karsh had been in his tangled, overgrown herb garden, tending to the special plants that helped him wage a valiant fight against his constant pain. He'd just picked enough to concoct the elixir he needed when, without warning, the immense lizard had swooped from the sky, snatched him in its monstrous claws, and carried him off — Karsh had dropped the seeds of his herbal remedy, spreading them over the landscape below.

Sometime later, Fredo delivered him to Thantos, unsure of what he had even accomplished by taking the tracker.

Enraged that Fredo had failed to deliver the twins, Thantos had quickly thought of a way to use his baby brother's "gift." He would use the elderly warlock to lure Ileana. Surely, she would rescue Karsh. And with the two of them out of the way, Camryn and Alexandra would be unprotected.

So far, it hadn't worked. But Thantos knew it would. He knew Ileana. For all her brilliance, her cunning, her beauty, bravery, even — at the bottom of it all — her pure heart, her downfall was what it had always been. Impatience.

She would not wait much longer to make her move.

Karsh knew what Thantos was thinking. He also knew a secret — one that neither of his captors realized he knew. Thantos might threaten Ileana, he might frighten, trick, and ultimately ensnare her. But he would not harm the talented young witch.

Which made Karsh think of someone else he once believed the hulking madman would never harm.

Thantos let out a deep, throaty laugh. "So, my lordship, you're still thinking of her after all these years. Interesting that you didn't scramble *that* thought; it was easy for me to read."

Karsh raised his raspy voice. "What did you do to her? Surely, in my incapacitated state, you can tell me. I am no threat to you."

Thantos stroked his dark, coarse beard. "Miranda, Miranda. What makes you think I had anything to do with the disappearance of my brother's wife?"

Fredo cut in, "Yeah, what makes you think she's alive? Besides, why do you care? Forget about her. She's gone, dead to you. You've got bigger problems."

Karsh blinked suddenly, as the thought, the *certainty*, washed over him. "Miranda's *not* dead, is she?"

Thantos abruptly sprang out his chair. Stopping just

short of the old man's nose, he seethed, "Know this: You will never see her alive again."

"Why is that, Lord Thantos?" Karsh challenged, unbowed and unafraid.

"Because, you stubborn, senile old trickster, if your ward, the charming Ileana, fails to come to your rescue, or delays much longer, you will be quite unable to see anyone ever again. You will be dead."

CHAPTER TEN
BRUISE CLUES

"Score!" Alex hooted triumphantly, flagging down her sister in the hallway between class periods the next day. "I've *got* something on her."

"You read Webb's mind?" Cam guessed eagerly.

"Better," Alex teased with a glint in her metallic eye. "I hid, I heard, I sent something crashing to the floor, I saw!"

Maybe it was seeing her sister so bummed. Or finding out that Webb was tangled up in Helping Hands — and had ensnared Beth. Perhaps it was Alex's plain prickliness at Karsh and Ileana for pulling a no-show.

Or, Alex thought, searching Cam's worried but hopeful face, most likely she just needed to help her sister, whether she agreed with Camryn or not. Whatever: Alex had decided to deal with Webb.

Her way.

Which meant, that morning, sneaking into the teachers' ladies' room, posting an OUT OF ORDER sign on a stall door, then locking herself in, pulling her knees up, so no one would notice her — and waiting.

Just after homeroom, her gambit paid off.

As she told Cam, "Turns out Cecilia Webb's got a cell phone, and either the reception in the bathroom is very good or during first period it's unlikely she'd be interrupted there. Anyway, as soon as she walked in, her phone was ringing. Only I guess she didn't get to it in time, 'cause she had to call back.

Cam added with a grin, "Who was she talking to?"

Alex shrugged. "Don't know."

Cam's smile faded. "But she was saying something totally incriminating, right?"

"Not unless you consider 'I miss you,' and 'Don't worry, honey, I'm going to come through for you' incriminating."

Cam folded her arms across her chest. "So she's got a boyfriend she hasn't seen in a while — that's it? *That's* what you scored?"

"That . . . and, uh, this little tidbit: He's in prison!"

Cam's jaw dropped. "He is? How'd you . . ."

Alex's eyes sparkled. "I got impatient waiting for her to say something more interesting. So I decided to see if the phone number of that 'missed call' showed up."

So, Cam thought, anti-cell-phone girl Alex had learned a thing or two about mobiles. About to give her sister props, Cam remembered, "But how'd you see the digital readout on the phone through the bathroom door?"

"I didn't," Alex told her. "Supersight is your department. But making her drop the phone — moving it to a spot where I could see it — that's kinda mine."

Impressed, Cam asked, "And you saw . . . what, Massachusetts State Prison?"

"Right. Like it was that easy! All I had time to do was hit 'List missed calls.' The first one that popped up was this phone number . . ."

"Which," Cam finished for her, "you looked up."

"State penitentiary, sista."

The fact that Webb was calling someone — her boyfriend, probably — in the pen was a juicy tidbit and a potential clue. But until they knew more, it wasn't enough evidence to nail her.

"Let's get some more!" Cam declared.

Unfortunately, more evidence of the Webb sort wasn't in huge supply that week, nor the one that followed.

It wasn't for lack of trying. Cam got ahold of the teacher's schedule, so the twins could "coincidentally" bump into her and Alex could get close enough to read her mind. They passed her in the hallway and on the stairwell. Once, they hovered nearby when Amanda stopped her to ask a question. The day Webb was on lunchroom duty, Alex made the ultimate sacrifice and ate in the cafeteria.

But at no moment, fleeting or extended, could Alex get in to Webb's head.

During lunch, while Webb was on cafeteria patrol, Cam slipped out of the building and made for the teachers' parking lot. Maybe there was some evidence in the scheming substitute's car that supersighted Cam could unearth.

Trying not to be conspicuous, Cam circled the black Acura with the Helping Hands bumper sticker, telescoping in on the contents. Webb wasn't much for neatness. On the passenger seat lay maps, Helping Hands brochures, and a box of tissues. Empty water bottles and fast-food containers littered the floor. The backseat was empty.

Cam was about to walk away when something wedged under the back of the driver's seat caught her eye. The corner of a sales receipt, so small that no one with normal eyesight could see it. Luckily, Cam wasn't in that category. She zoomed in. It appeared to be from a cheapo jewelry store in Boston called Trompe L'Oeil. And — whoa! — Webb had bought, like, a dozen different items. Only . . . Cam's eyes began to sting as she telescoped in more carefully. Try as she might, she couldn't read the signature. Only that it didn't say Cecilia Webb. The first initial was a B. The last name began with an R.

The receipt was potentially interesting, but how it — or the call from prison — tied her to some shoplifting ring, Cam couldn't figure.

Meanwhile, during class Ms. Webb continued her demanding, demeaning manner, tossing out rapid-fire questions, piling on the homework. But after a while the class's griping trickled to a halt. Most people adjusted. One student in particular seemed even to blossom under the tough tactics of their substitute: Elisabeth Fish.

Beth had become superstudent, racking up one Einstein moment after another. Her homework assignments were so exemplary, Webb read them aloud a couple of times. Pop quizzes, the scourge of Cam's existence, seemed to be what Beth lived for.

There was a flip side to the academic coin: Beth's zoom up the GPA ladder in social studies mirrored her slip-slide in nearly every other subject. According to a round of Six Pack IMs, Kristen noted that Beth, usually her closest competitor in Spanish, had totally messed up on the last test. Amanda wrote, In algebra, she was marked unprepared. I don't think she did the homework. Sukari typed, Dag, and I thought it was just a temporary case of brain rot when the girl formerly known as Ms. Frizzle couldn't come up with the formula for iodine.

Beth was not on the IM tip. She wasn't anywhere with the Six Pack lately. She bagged their Friday pizza fest, bailed on the mall troll and movies on Saturday. She was barely on-line anymore. E-mails went unanswered, some unread even. And when the talk of the school was a round of shopliftings at the Galleria — another scam involving a teen and a decoy adult — Beth noticeably didn't participate.

As Cam feared, Beth hadn't shown up for two soccer practices and was booted off the team. Worse, her friend didn't seem to care. During lunch one day, she got defensive about Helping Hands. Volunteering was so time-intensive that Amanda, who'd meant to sign up, had changed her mind. And Beth (so unlike her) had taken the innocent girl to task. "I guess helping abandoned children isn't as important to you as you thought it was," she'd said, sniffing.

Amanda defended herself. "That's not fair. Ms. Webb said we'd have to meet after school every day. Learn fund-raising techniques, look up potential donors on the Internet, design flyers and stuff. You've been doing all that, and you haven't even *seen* the kids. I would have no time for anything else. I've already made a commitment to soccer and my team needs me."

"And your friends need you" is what Cam wanted to say to Beth, but didn't. Their relationship was still on the fritz. Cam didn't want it to sputter out.

It wasn't until the following Saturday morning, when emptying her backpack in search of her English notes, that Cam found the folded-up piece of paper she'd wedged into her math textbook.

I need to talk to you. Alone. Really crucial stuff going on. Call me on my cell phone right after school.

Beth's note. The date was a week and a half ago.

Beth seemed surprised, and not especially happy, to see Cam standing at her front door a little after ten A.M. on Saturday morning. Still in her pj's, without her contacts in, her hair a dense tangle of bed-head frizz, she squinted suspiciously. "What are you doing here?"

Feeling suddenly awkward, Cam folded her arms. "I need to see you. And I figured even Helping Hands wouldn't have you up and out this early."

"You should have called," Beth mumbled. "This is really not a great time."

From inside the house, Cam could hear muffled sounds: a dog barking, music coming from Beth's sister

Lauren's room, voices raised in anger. She'd assumed the TV was on, but now realized the voices belonged to Beth's parents.

Cam aimed for a quip. "Nothing like a little family discord with your Cheerios, huh?"

Beth's face darkened as if she was about to say something, but she bit her lip instead.

"Can we go to your room?" Cam took a step inside. "This is important, Bethie."

Her friend didn't answer, but turned, motioning for Cam to follow. At least Beth wasn't that mad, Cam thought with relief as the girls walked down the hallway to the back of the house; she hadn't booted her.

Beth's room was bright and sunny, a shrine to friendship, flora, and fauna — a total reflection of the good-natured girl's personality. Ceramic vases holding bunches of dried flowers dotted the room; Sierra Club posters fought with collages and family photos for wall space. Snapshots of the Six Pack were everywhere, a friendship captured through the years. Cam noticed Beth's Mary Englebreit sappy-saying calendar was still on the month before.

As Beth was about to close the door, her dog, a wire-haired fox terrier — the canine equivalent of Beth, Cam used to secretly think — named Cooper, bounded into the room and jumped onto Beth's still unmade bed.

Cam plopped down next to him and massaged him behind the ears. "Hey, Coop, what's the scoop?"

Beth pulled her hair back in a scrunchie and sat down at her desk to put her contacts in.

"So, anyway, we need to talk," Cam said finally.

"Fine," Beth said in a flat voice, propping one eye open while she inserted a lens. "You've clearly got a bone, so pick."

Disappointed that her friend had not warmed up more, Cam plunged ahead. "Look, I'm not exactly sure what happened between us, but I guess it probably seems like I haven't been the greatest friend to you."

"Gee, what makes you say that?" Beth cracked as she slipped the other contact in and blinked. "Just because you see me doing something on my own and feel the need to stop me?"

"It's not that and you know it —" Cam started to protest.

But Beth interrupted, "Or maybe it's that I'm doing better than you are in *one subject,* and you can't stand it? Or is it that Cami's not teacher's pet?"

Teacher's nightmare is what Cam wanted to say. "Don't be like that. I . . . look, I've been distracted lately, and I just got your note."

"My note?" Beth seemed really surprised. *"That's* why you're here? So over, Camryn."

Guiltily, Cam ventured, "Whatever the problem was, it's been solved? You don't need to talk to me?"

"Let's just say I've found other people to talk to."

Stung, a sharp breath caught in Cam's throat. "I'm . . . I'm really sorry. But that's not the only reason I came over."

Beth guessed, "You want to try and talk me out of doing the one thing that's meaningful to me now. Wow — great friend you're being!"

"I know you're angry. And maybe you have a right to be. But that doesn't change the fact that I still care about you. I worry about you."

"What's to worry about?" Beth challenged. "I'm helping children."

Cam pressed on. "Social studies aside, you're messing up in school. We never see you anymore, we barely hear from you. You are still my BFF no matter what." She paused, then added quietly, "I miss you."

Beth turned away to grab a tissue and blot her eye. Was it the contacts, or was her friend tearing up?

"BFF. Right." Beth sniffed. "I think a certain punky lookalike has taken over that position."

Although she heard the hurt in her friend's voice, Cam tried for another quip. "Like they say, 'You can pick your friends, but you can't pick your long-lost identical twin.' Or something. You and I picked each other a long time ago."

Beth's lip trembled and she swiveled in her chair to face Cam. "I've missed you, too. But Helping Hands is a good thing in my life. Other stuff is going on. I've been trying to tell you . . . but you weren't listening."

Now it was Cam's turn to tear up. "I'm listening now."

"Elisabeth!" The door flew open with a bang, and Beth's mother appeared, eyes puffy, cheeks red — completely frazzled.

Beth leaped out of her chair and darted in front of her mother, as if trying to shield Cam from her. "Mom, what is it? We're kind of in the middle of something. . . ."

Mrs. Fish seemed to be flying apart at the seams. "My necklace is missing! Did you borrow it and forget to tell me?"

Beth shook her head. "No. Mom, Cam and I were talking. Did you ask Lauren?"

But her mom wouldn't be put off. "She doesn't have it. It's the diamond one that Grandma Godlen gave me. It's worth . . . well . . . are you sure?"

Beth put her arm around her mother's waist and led her to the door. "Give me a half hour. Then Lauren and I will help you look for it."

Cam couldn't help what came out of her mouth next, the minute the door closed. She hadn't meant to sound accusing. "Beth, you're not, you know, donating your mom's jewelry or anything? For the cause . . . Helping Hands, I mean?"

Her friend was startled. "You think I would do that?"

Cam hesitated. "The Beth I know? No way. But lately, you're just, you've been acting strangely."

"Maybe the Beth you know is changing. Maybe it's about time. Maybe I have my own interests that aren't the same as yours. But it doesn't mean I'd do anything . . . radical."

Cam couldn't let it go. "It just feels like you're doing things you'll regret because you're upset about our friendship, about Alex."

Beth paused. Then quietly she said, "Why do you always think everything's about you? Do you even have a clue how self-centered you are?"

It was Cam's turn to be startled. "That's not fair. If you saw me doing — like being self-destructive — I would hope you'd be there. You always have. Being a friend is being able to say what's really on your mind, acting on it."

Beth countered, "Being a friend is being able to see things differently once in a while. Accepting change. Look, okay, so I messed up this week in a few classes, it's not the end of the world. I've been busy. I really believe in what Helping Hands is doing. I don't understand why you can't accept that. And if you can't, maybe it is time to reevaluate our friendship. Move on, even."

Cam walked over to where Beth was sitting, and knelt so they'd be eye to eye. "I don't want that. I hope you don't, either."

Beth blinked back tears. "How could you accuse me . . . ?"

"My bad. That was —" She paused. "Way out of line. Forgive?" She pulled a tissue out of the flowered box on the desk and handed it to her.

Beth blew her nose. "And forgotten."

Because she still couldn't tell Beth the truth about Ms. Webb and the shoplifting, Cam searched for a neutral topic. "So anyway, you're still going to the winter dance tonight, right?"

"I'll be there," Beth assured her. For the first time that morning, a trace of her usually bright smile played on her lips.

Which gave Cam an idea. "Hey, you want to double? Go together? It's short notice, but Jason's friend Rick is kinda cool. . . ."

Beth's smile dissolved. She shook her head. "Nothing ever changes, does it? What makes you think I need you to get me a date?"

Cam blanched. "I don't think that. You said you didn't have one."

"That was two weeks ago."

"Of course I don't need to get you a date. You're totally fine going solo. . . . Sukari is and —"

Beth interrupted her. "I would be fine going on my own, but it so happens I have a date."

"You do?"

"Try to keep the shock out of your voice, okay, Cami?"

"I'm surprised you didn't tell me, that's all."

She shouldn't have been. Apparently, there was lots Beth hadn't been sharing lately. "So, what's he like? Who is he? Is he . . . you know, a cool guy?"

Even as the words tumbled out, instantly Cam knew he wasn't. For, as Beth started to happily tell her about this new boy in her life, Cam felt it: an icy chill, a throbbing in her temples, goose bumps. And she saw . . .

Tall and ripped, with milk-chocolate-brown eyes framed by long dark lashes, a shock of tousled light brown hair, a killer smile.

"Shane," they said at the same time.

The boy from the Helping Hands cart. Of course, Beth would have been working with him. Shane Wright.

Somehow, Cam knew he was all wrong.

CHAPTER ELEVEN
ONE FATHER TOO MANY

Alex lay in bed, arms akimbo, staring at the ceiling. The alarm clock's digital readout told her it was late, 10:17 A.M., still, she didn't want to get up. For the first time in a long time, she was alone.

Cam had rushed off to see Beth. The silence coming from Dylan's room —. connected to hers by the bath/laundry room combo — told her he was asleep. The 'rents, Dave and Emily, would not disturb her.

She'd been dreaming and wished she could will herself back into it, let the sweet feelings wash over her. She pictured piecing together the dream-fragments, weaving a soft downy blanket, wrapping herself in it.

She was in Montana. Outside, the mountain air,

clear and pinprick brisk, nipped at her cheeks. Outside, the vivid colors, the deep foresty green of the leaves, the blinding white of the snowcapped mountains, the azure blue of the sky; mornings that looked like someone had taken a giant paintbrush and swabbed strokes of orange, yellow, red. Big-sky country. Yeah.

And inside. Inside her home it was warm, the sweet aroma of hotcakes or eggs and bacon wafting from the kitchen licked playfully at her nose, made her salivate. Sara, sunny-side-up, smart, and loving, humming softly off-key. Sara smiling.

The friends, funny, loyal Lucinda with her round face and puckish lips, and sweet daydreamer Evan — he of the dreadlocks and smart, wry sense of humor — would soon call for her. She knew how it looked to most kids at Big Sky Regional: They were outsiders, a tight trio who didn't fit in with any group. No one "got" them. But that didn't matter, because they got one another. Together, they worked at after-school jobs, they leaned on one another, hung together, held on for dear life. And the game they played most often was "anywhere but here."

Back in Montana, it was familiar, it was safe. No one was after her, no one was trying to lure her. No one was trying to kill her.

She was home.

Alex flipped over on the bed, let her arm dangle off the side. It wasn't working. She could not willpower herself back into the dream. The pain-in-the-"buts" of reality plucked at her, nudging her awake.

But: Montana winters were bitter. Especially when they didn't have enough money to pay the heat bill. One bad time her goldfish had frozen to death. In the hollow of winter, trees were bare; the snow turned to gray mush, the sky black and foreboding.

But: Sara smoked. The sweet aroma of breakfast was forever mixed with the bitter fumes of cigarettes.

But: Her mobile home was a tin box, and there *was* a villain in the piece, who was "after" both of them. The rancid landlord, Hardy Beeson, unceasing in his efforts to evict them. His weapon of choice: plain meanness. Her friends didn't have it any easier than she did. Luce was a sweet dreamer living in a matchbox house among too many needy relatives; Evan's mom drank too much.

Alex's friends were her world, but there was so much she couldn't share with them. Her ability to move stuff, to hear what people were thinking. Her weirdness.

Except for Sara — when she was healthy, not at the end — it wasn't better back there.

Alex rolled onto her side and opened her eyes. Cam's room, now their room. Sherbet colors, soft pinks, mint greens, baby blues. Shelves lined with books, CDs, photographs, candles. Twin beds, a shared night table between then, twin desks. Someone — Cam — had made room for her here.

This was home.

Yawning loudly, Alex threw off the covers, swung her legs over the bed, got up, and took a shower. Even though there was no danger of the hot water running out, as happened so often back home, she kept it short. Old habits would take time to break.

Speaking of habits, Alex thought, surveying the bedroom, Cami had a bad one, especially when she was in a rush. Slob-o girl had left the contents of her upended backpack all over the floor, as well as piles of clothes, representing everything she'd worn during the week, mixed with everything she'd been thinking of wearing. And was thinking of wearing for the school dance tonight. A cheesy, cutesy scene Alex was so not making. Besides, Cade Richman, the cute guy she sort of liked — okay, *did* like — wasn't going. He was out of town that weekend, visiting his sister at her new college.

A bolt of do-good inspiration hit Alex, a random act of neatness. After getting dressed, she began to clean up. It was when she tossed Cam's wrinkled T-shirts in the laundry basket that it happened.

The odor hit her. Sharp, sickening, and familiar. It smelled like death, Sara's death. Alex pulled everything out of the basket quickly, although she knew exactly what she was looking for.

A pair of jeans. She held them up and almost barfed.

Without thinking, Alex threw open the door that connected to Dylan's room and stormed in. It was all she could do to stifle the urge to scream at him — but even blind rage had its insight. Alerting Dave and Emily was not the move right now. So she settled for grabbing sleepy-boy's arm and shaking him awake.

Unsurprisingly, he didn't appreciate it.

"Wha . . . what's going on? What is it?" Dylan's light blue eyes flew open in panic. Alex heard his heart pounding wildly.

"Get up!" she demanded.

"Is there a fire? What's happening?" Dylan yelped in alarm.

"There's no fire," Alex retorted, "but you're toast."

Dylan propped himself up on his elbows, wide-eyed, his heart still thumping — Alex had no trouble busting into his head. *What's up with sista? She's gone berserk! Why's she in my face?*

"You want something in your face?" Alex threw the jeans at him.

With a quick swipe, Dylan deflected the denim. "Dude, I don't know what's up with you, but . . ."

"Then let me spell it out for you, *dude*! This reeks! You've been smoking. That's why sista's in your face!"

If he were awake and clearheaded, he might have realized she'd read his mind.

Dylan sat up straight. He lifted the telltale jeans. "So you smell smoke on these. So what?"

Alex narrowed her fiery eyes, wishing she had Cam's power — she'd set the nicotine jeans on fire.

"If I can smell it, so can your mother! What do you think she's gonna do when she finds out?"

Dylan suddenly sprang off the bed and barreled by Alex. "Hey, man, you're not my mother, so lay off! And so what if I've had a couple. I thought you were cool."

"I am cool. More than you know. Do not do this, Dudley."

Dylan ran his fingers through his clumped-together bed-head spikes. "You're making a big thing out of nothing. It was, like, one cigarette."

Although she was a full head shorter than he, Alex blocked his way to the bathroom. "Don't you get it? It's addictive!"

"Thanks for the PSA," Dylan grumbled.

Alex backed off. Confrontation was getting her nowhere. "Wait, Dyl," she said, her voice softening. "I didn't mean to go ballistic, but this is crazy-making for me."

"Look, I'm not gonna croak like your old lady, if that's what you're freaked about."

Alex was horrified.

Dylan, instantly ashamed.

There was a knock at the door, but she and Dylan just stood there, staring at each other, speechless.

Another knock, louder this time. Accompanied by Dave's voice. "Alex? Are you in there?"

The door opened slowly and Dave peeked in. Clearly, he realized he'd stumbled into something unpretty, but said only, "I need you downstairs, Alex. Sorry to interrupt."

Staring hard at Dylan, Alex said, "It's fine. We're done here."

Alex wondered if her summons might be for a scolding: If Emily knew about Dylan's new habit, she'd blame Alex. Now *that,* Alanis, is ironic. But as she turned into the kitchen where Emily was waiting, arms crossed, Alex knew it was something else entirely.

"Why don't we sit down?" Dave settled into a chair at the small square kitchen table.

Guardedly, Alex followed. A second later, so did Emily.

Alex didn't have to read their minds, she could read their faces. Both were confused and concerned.

"So." Alex drummed her fingers on the table. "What the dilly-yo, guys? What'd I do this time?"

Dave cleared his throat. "You didn't do anything —"

Emily interrupted, "It's what you didn't do. Or didn't say."

Dave coughed. "We don't want to make this into anything more than what it probably is. . . ."

Alex could feel the chip settling squarely on her shoulder. "So *probably* . . . what is it that I didn't do?"

Dave propped his wire-rimmed glasses on the bridge of his nose. "We got some upsetting news this morning."

"If it's about Dyl —" Alex started, but was stopped dead in her tracks by Emily's next words.

"About the guardianship."

Alex tightened. Was it not going through?

Dave put his hand on her shoulder. Alex shook it off.

"Let's not panic," he said, ignoring her diss. "We've run into a little glitch is all." He stopped, as if to measure her reaction.

Emily jumped in, "A FedEx package was delivered to the office this morning. There's something you haven't told us."

If you only knew what I haven't told you — like everything, Alex thought. She eyed Emily. Was Cam's mom trying to hide the relief on her face? Maybe she *wants* a glitch, so she can get me out of here, and they can go back to dinner at this four-seater table. But when she felt Dave's hand on her shoulder again, warm and reassuring, she realized this truly good man was genuinely upset. That was the moment the chip slid off.

"Alex, we have to ask you something," Dave said slowly. "And we need you to be totally honest."

"Go for it," she mumbled, hiding her rising panic.

"According to the papers in the package, our guardianship is being contested."

Alex's puzzled "By who?" was drowned out by Emily's terse, "By a man who says he's your father . . ."

Aron? He's alive? Alex thought, or might have even said.

No. The next words out of Dave's mouth threw her for a head-spinning loop. "An Isaac Fielding, husband of Sara. Alex, you told us he was dead."

Alex's hand had flown to her face at the mention of Ike Fielding; her startling gray eyes — unnerving replicas of Cam's — grew wide. And Alex had bolted.

Emily wanted to go after her. On her way out the door, Alex heard her protest, "No, Dave, she just can't run away from this conversation. She owes us an explanation."

And Dave's calm rejoinder, "I know. But let's give

108————————————

her some space. The kid is obviously shocked. Maybe she really believed he was dead."

"Or maybe what she believes is that she can fabricate any story that suits her, we're that gullible. . . ."

Alex ran to the garage, grabbed Dylan's mountain bike — another of his castoffs she'd gotten custody of — and pedaled as fast as she could. She wished for a shut-off switch to her hyperhearing. She didn't want to know what Emily and Dave were saying. She just needed to think. And for that, she needed a private place.

Half Moon Cove was a tiny crescent-shaped slice of beach, not far from Cam's house. It was protected from the street by a waist-high cobblestone seawall. Because it was on the bay, not the ocean, the water was fairly calm and shallow — not unlike a lake beach, the kind found in landlocked places. Like Montana.

It was the one place in Marble Bay that reminded Alex of home.

Cam parked her bike against a tree. She was the only person who could figure out where Alex had gone. She scurried down the stone steps to the pebbly beach and heard it. She stopped and listened.

Why's Ike showing up now? I bet I know what he wants from me. They can't make me go with him. I can't. I won't. . . . I'll run away!

If you run away, Cam said telepathically as she scanned the beach, looking for Alex, *I'll have to come with. . . . We're attached now.*

But Alex wasn't in a joking mood. She shot back, *I can just see the headlines in the* Marble Bay Buccaneer, *or whatever cutesy name you have for the local paper: Princess Abandons Perfect Life; Alpha Girl Goes AWOL . . . Goal-den Girl Goes out of Bounds. Like you'd do that.*

"For you I would." Cam said that aloud as she finally came upon Alex, sitting with her back pressed against the seawall, staring out into the bay.

Alex looked up warily. "I wouldn't ask you to. And in related news, I didn't ask for company right now, either." Wearing thin cargo pants and a tank top, the girl was shivering.

Cam, in a sweater set, slipped out of her cardigan and draped it around her twin's shoulders. "I come uninvited. Adjust."

In auto-reject mode, Alex was about to toss the sweater off her shoulders, but thought better of it. Caving, she pulled it tight around her instead. "Thanks for the cover-up, but what I need right now is my space. Go."

"Why'd you run out?" Cam asked, ignoring Alex's dismissal and sliding down next to her in the sand.

Alex shrugged. "Seemed like a good idea at the time."

Cam remembered the saying on Beth's calendar, and quipped, "Wherever you go, there you are."

Alex threw back her head. "Thanks, Mary Englebreit. When I need a cheesy cliché, I'll know whose brain to tap into."

In truth, they both knew why she'd bolted. It wasn't because Dave and Emily had caught her in a lie. It was simply because she was scared to death.

"Als," Cam continued gently, "why'd you lie in the first place?"

"I didn't," Alex stubbornly insisted.

"The night you arrived at my doorstep, when my parents were trying to figure out what was going on, you said he was dead."

"You're not the only one with a super memory, ginkgo biloba girl." Alex stuck out her chin defiantly. "As I recall, it was Dave who said — and I quote — 'You just lost your mom. Your dad died some years ago.'"

"Ixnay on the quibbling, Alex. He was repeating what you led us to believe."

Alex turned away. She didn't want Cam to see her — and she certainly didn't want to see a reflection of her own face, worried, caring about her.

"You knew he was alive," Cam repeated.

"To me, he is dead. I mean, for all the good he ever

was. It never occurred to me he would come looking for me — or want me."

"So what's your hypothesis — why's he suddenly in the picture?" Cam asked.

Alex grew angry. "Why? Let's see, let me channel Ike — the little I remember. Hey, Sara's dead. That could mean insurance money. I bet the kid has it! I could use it. . . ."

Cam put a comforting arm around her sister. "Maybe he's changed? People do, you know."

"He's not people. He's . . . he's the human equivalent of landfill. He's . . . he walked out on us, Cam. Left us with nothing but a ton of bills, debt that my mother could never climb out of. Poverty." She didn't say, but thought, *Nothing you would know about, with your perfect loving family.*

Cam closed her eyes and thought for a moment. "If you let them, Alex, my 'perfect loving family,' as you sarcastically call them, could be yours, too. They want to try and make it work."

Alex kicked the sand and blurted, "Your mom doesn't. She'd be just as happy to send me back. To him."

Loudly, Cam made the sound of a buzzer. "Wrong! Emily can be tightly wound, but she's got a good heart. The best heart. Don't believe me, break into her thoughts. . . ."

Alex chilled at the thought.

"I dare you!" Cam challenged. "Anyway, you can't doubt my dad. Like Karsh told us, Dave was chosen to be my adoptive dad. And he wouldn't have been if he didn't have our best interests at heart."

"Dave signed on for one superpowered kid. Not two," Alex reminded her.

Suddenly, a thought caught Cam unbidden, and she blurted, "How messed up is this? Our biological dad was Aron. A good and powerful warlock, but a dead one all the same."

Alex instantly caught on. "Ike, a bad and lazy loser, was never my dad, but suddenly, he returns *from* the 'dead,' wanting to be!"

Cam continued, "Dave raised me; he wants to be there for both of us."

Alex added, "Emily didn't give birth to you; Sara didn't give birth to me — but they both were moms, in every way that counts."

"Still, our birth mother is Miranda . . ." Cam stopped, not knowing how to end that sentence. Then she exclaimed, "Parents! Oh, man — you can't live with 'em, can't live without 'em."

Alex cracked up.

Cam stood, brushed herself off, and extended her hand. After a split second, Alex grasped it and allowed Cam to pull her up.

"Here's what we do. And don't say 'bad plan, Cam' 'cause it's a good one. We go home and download Dad about Ike-the-unlikable. Dad schedules a legal hearing; we fight this."

"You think that'd work?" Alex asked tentatively, afraid to be hopeful.

"Ike can't have you. End of story. We are stuck with you, Alexandra Fielding!"

Alex grinned large. "Dude, you should be so lucky."

CHAPTER TWELVE
AN ENCHANTED EVENING

Cam did a double take when she and Jason got to the dance that night. Score one for Bree! And Kristen, always the most artistic of her friends, and the whole decorating committee. What was once "Everygym" had truly been transformed into a dazzling winter wonderland. The whole room seemed to sparkle and glisten.

Silver and white twinkling stars hung from the rafters. Mylar balloons had been attached to the light fixtures, white curlicue streamers wound around the pipes that crisscrossed the exposed ceiling beams. Faux snow, like the kind used in the movies, was sprinkled throughout, practically covering the gym floor. Cam bet Bree had used her Hollywood connections to get it.

Snow-scene murals wrapped around the walls. The basketball hoops had been draped with ice skates and old-fashioned sleigh bells.

But what tickled Cam the most were the life-size snowmen posted around the room. Made of giant Styrofoam balls, each wore a silly scarf and funny hat.

"Oh, man! This place rocks!" Jason exclaimed, taking everything in.

Cam looked up into his twinkling dark chocolate eyes. "Best school dance you've been to?"

"For more reasons than one." Jason tried to sound casual, but he couldn't hide his happiness as he slipped his arm around Cam's waist. "In case I didn't say it before, you look, you know, really nice. Great."

Cam lit up. "You did say it before — but you can be repeat-o boy." Between the trauma-ramas with Beth and Alex, Cam had barely had time to think about what to wear. She ended up with a sparkly silver halter top over a leather miniskirt. On a last-minute impulse, she'd swapped her sun necklace for a loop-chain lariat.

"Let's check out the foodstuffs," Jason was saying, pointing to the far end of the gym, where long tables had been set up with a worthy smorgasbord.

Cam could see a crowd already there. By their motions, she could tell they were making fun of Mrs. Sullivan's leaden meatballs, the ones she made every year. The joke was, you ate one and stayed glued to the floor — it felt like a ten-pound cannonball in your gut.

"Cami! Over here," Amanda called out with a wave.

Cam smiled. 'Manda was in a powder-blue ankle-length peasant skirt and striped tube wrap top, her carrot-colored ringlets framing her baby-doll face. She started off toward her friend, when Rick, one of Jason's friends, called from across the room, "Over here, man, check this out." He was at the buffet, juggling three meatballs.

"Be right back." Jason gave Cam's bare shoulder a light squeeze as he headed over toward Rick.

"Where's everyone else?" Cam asked Amanda.

"Sukari's over there." Amanda pointed to the far end of the gym, where Sukari, outstanding in a peach wrap dress with matching sash, stood, surrounded by a group — most of whom were guys.

"Trolling for hunks, she didn't waste any time!" Cam laughed, giving Sukari props. "Although that *is* a lot of boyage, even for her."

Amanda tilted her head. "Should I go and even the odds?"

"Excellent plan," Cam agreed with a smile, suddenly wishing Dylan and Alex were there. But Dylan had made other plans, and her twin had insisted she was not school-dance girl. Cam hadn't pushed it.

She might have, however, if she'd known then what she suddenly knew now.

Something toxic had seeped into the room.

She felt it seconds before she saw it. Cam spun around, and her hunch was instantly confirmed. Ms. Webb was chaperoning the dance. Catching Cam's eye on her, she had the nerve to smile! But the smile was pure . . .

"Evil! Wicked outfit, glam-Cam!" Brianna, in a barely there black slip dress with spaghetti straps, accosted her. "Flash of fashion-forward brilliance to pair last year's mini with a halter top from five minutes ago."

Was that a diss? A compliment? Whatever. She pulled Bree over, motioned to Webb, and whispered, "What's *she* doing chaperoning?"

"I would know this, exactly why?" Bree shrugged.

"You know everything," Cam insisted, "You're ultimate insider girl."

"Kudos accepted, for that *and* for the extraordinary gym decor," Bree deadpanned. "But for some reason, who's chaperoning didn't even make my 'to obsess about' list."

Kristen, her long, black hair flowing over a pink sheath, flounced over. "You guys! Beth just got here — and you gotta see this!"

Cam and Bree turned toward the entrance to the gym. There was only one word for Elisabeth Fish right now: luminous! A total Cinderella-at-the-ball as if a spot-light shone on the girl, and she simply dazzled.

Since the morning, Beth's hair had morphed from astonished frizz to a princesslike cascade of tight and shiny curls. She wore a strapless rose-patterned dress, which set off her beaming megawatt smile.

But it was her main accessory that rocked the dance: her date.

Shane threw off a smooth, sure-of-himself vibe. Was it because he looked so incredibly hot that Cam's pulse raced? Or was her anxiety uptick caused by something else?

Like a synchronized swim team, the Six Pack, plus dates and friends, swooped around Beth and Shane all at once.

"You glow, girl!" Sukari high-fived her.

Amanda added, "Your inner light is definitely on halogen."

Brianna cut to the chase. Holding a diamond-braceleted hand out to Beth's date, she chirped, "Hi! I'm Brianna. And you're Shane. No doubt."

He grinned and shook her hand. "No doubt."

In default flirt mode, Bree purred, "Naturally Bethie mentioned you, but she never said you were so —"

"Tall," Kristen cut her off with a kick to her ankle. "You seem taller than we . . . uh, expected . . ."

To Cam, Shane seemed amused. Not uncomfortable, as Jason — or most guys — would have been in this situation. Not unlike he was at the mall that day when she accidentally slammed into him.

Beth did the intros, ending with, "And you've already met Camryn, of course."

"*That is* Camryn Barnes," he playfully teased, just as he had that first time. "Who could forget?" He didn't move to take her hand. Instead, he squeezed Beth's hand tighter and leaned over, brushing his lips across Beth's temple.

Cam was suddenly reminded of the time, back when she and Beth were kids, that they'd been tickled by a silly pun. Because of Beth's last name, it used to reduce them to instant giggle fits. "You can tune a piano, but you can't tune a Fish." This guy's got her tune all right, Cam now thought.

You think I'm playing her?

Cam gasped and choked back her words. Shane had read her mind.

The dance was ruined. Even though the band had cranked up, Jason was by her side again, and voices, music, and laughter reverberated from floor to ceiling to walls, Cam couldn't keep her mind off Shane.

Every time she turned around, Cecilia Webb stared

back. Was the woman stalking her? Waiting to pounce? Could she read Cam's mind, too? Most chilling of all, could there be a connection between Shane and Webb?

Cam had arrived at the dance feeling like her old carefree self, surrounded by her friends, with a cute guy, looking good. Now, two hours into it, she was on edge.

It wasn't until the band launched into a raucous version of "Old Time Rock 'n' Roll" that she went over the edge.

Bam! There it was: Her heart pounded, beads of perspiration broke out on her forehead, that sickeningly familiar icy chill swirled around her.

Instinctively, her hand went to her throat. Her fingers found not the chain of her sun necklace, but the lariat instead. She whirled around, her back to Jason now. She knew who was the likely cause of her premonition, but had no clue *what* was about to happen. Only that it was bad.

"Was it something I sang — off-key?" Jason leaned in close to be heard over the music.

Turning around, Cam giggled nervously. "No, it's just I —"

He touched her arm. "Want to get out of here?"

"— need to get some water," she finished, feeling pulled, magnetlike, to the other side of the dance floor.

"Want company?" he offered.

"That's okay," Cam quickly dissuaded him. "Be right back."

Acting on pure instinct, she bolted to the far corner of the gym. There, the tallest of the decorative snowmen had been posted. Like a sentry keeping guard, it stood in front of the door leading to the equipment room. Without thinking, Cam brushed by the snowman and rushed through the door. It didn't occur to her to wonder why it was unlocked. She knew: Whoever was after her would follow.

"So, we meet again. *That is* Camryn Barnes."

His voice was light, teasing. He'd been waiting for her.

She heard the door swing closed behind her and struggled to keep cool. "As if any of our meetings," she responded, "have been exactly accidental."

Shane's playful eyes glinted. "Accidentally-on-purpose, then?"

Cam searched his face for a clue to his real identity — and his agenda. An unexpected calm settled over her. Her pulse slowed to normal; she no longer felt chilled. In fact, she began to feel a strange comfort in his presence.

Then she thought of Beth.

Cam stuck out her chin. No matter who he was, or

what he wanted, she could deal. Even without Alex, or her necklace — without any word, even, from her protectors — she was no helpless victim. "What do you want with me, Shane? Were you sent here —"

"To convert you?"

For a second, Cam was confused. Convert her? To what? Was he talking about . . . Helping Hands?

Shane laughed. "You can't still think this is about . . . charity?"

He'd tapped into her brain again. Okay. She could handle this. "So you're a mind reader." She shrugged and went all Shania Twain. "That don't impress me much. What else can you do?"

Shane said, "All sorts of things. Come with me and find out."

"Where?"

"Coventry Island. That's where we live."

"Where's that?" Cam was interested in spite of herself. "I mean, is it on . . ." She wanted to say, "Earth," but how dumb did that sound? "Is it a real place?"

Shane laughed and his eyes twinkled. "It's off the coast of Wisconsin, in Lake Superior. Real enough for you?"

Go with him — to some remote island? Neh-*vuh*! She shook her head. "I'm here now, Shane. Or whatever your real name is."

"Actually, it is Shane. My parents were big Western movie fans."

"Fine, Shane. Whatever message you have to deliver, do it here, or forever hold your —"

Something wasn't right. Had the door behind her opened? Was Ms. Webb about to join them? Would it be two against one? Cam wished she had Alex's hyperhearing! She listened harder, but now heard nothing.

"Peace? Forever hold my peace?" he finished her sentence. "Interesting thing about peace. You might never find it, until you know who you really are." He paused, then his eyes bored into her, and he added, "Don't you agree? Apolla?"

Cam swallowed hard, but fought to stay focused. He wasn't telling her anything she hadn't just deduced. Shane was a warlock, the latest messenger sent by "Uncle" Thantos. But where did Ms. Webb fit in? And what was the connection to Helping Hands?

"Lots of questions!" He'd read her mind again. "And of course, smart little witch that you are, you've already figured out some of it. But here's what you haven't figured out. I'm not here to hurt you. Or to kidnap you. I'm here on behalf of some people who've been waiting a long time to get to know you. So as your charming friend Beth might put it — 'Come with?' "

At the mention of her friend, Cam's hands went clammy, and her heart began to thud all over again.

"Leave Beth out of this. Stay away from her!"

Shane shrugged. "Beth is sweet. And idealistic. Unlike you, trusting. You could take a lesson, Apolla."

"I should trust you?!" In spite of her fear, Cam almost burst out laughing.

Shane leaned in and let his hands rest on her shoulders. At his touch, she felt a familiar jolt, a sensation that felt electric, exciting. He whispered, "Hey, Cam? Despite what you might think, I'm not the bad guy. I'm not evil. I'm doing the right thing."

"What *are* you doing, Shane? You still haven't answered me." That came out shakily.

"I'm here to take you where you really want to go, Apolla. To Coventry Island, where you were born, where your family is waiting. Your real family."

The room slowly began to spin. Cam grabbed onto a shelf to steady herself. She heard him saying, "You know you want to. You've always wanted to. They're all waiting for you. . . ."

But the next words weren't his. *Not like this. Not this way.* Alex! That's what Alex had said, the last time someone had tried to lure them. It was one against one. Cam had not seen Shane's powers in action, so she was not sure she could take him. She decided not to fight.

But she could bargain.

Gripping the edge of the shelf so hard her knuckles went white, Cam took a deep breath. She faced Shane straight on. "Deal. I'll come —"

"I knew you would!" He was pleased.

"On one condition."

"You have a condition?" His eyebrows shot up.

"Stay away from Beth. Just disappear — don't come back."

"But that would hurt her," Shane said softly.

"You're right and you're wrong. She is idealistic. And innocent. And no matter what you think you believe, you *are* the bad guy, Shane. It's bad to use Beth to get to me. So go ahead, break her heart — but not her spirit; don't mess with her soul."

For a split second, real empathy flashed across Shane's smooth face. He softened.

And in that split second, a plan came to Cam. But before she could put it into motion, the door behind her flew open.

CHAPTER THIRTEEN
THE NIGHTMARE

Three white orbs filled the archway: the snowman?! In her confusion, Cam thought it had walked and opened the door itself. But that wasn't —

"Grab her!" a voice coming from the snowman hissed. It was a voice she'd heard before.

Cam hadn't planned what to do next. She focused her blazing eyes on the Styrofoam snowman, trying to see inside it. She hadn't meant to scorch it — but suddenly, tendrils of smoke encircled the snowman and the acrid odor of charred Styrofoam swirled around them and began to seep swiftly into the gym beyond.

"Dumb move, Cam!" Shane didn't bother to hide his panic, as the smoke began to thicken.

"Stupid servant boy!" That voice again, thin and reedy. "Why are you wasting time? Just get her!" With that, a form leaped out from behind the snowman: a man with a swizzle-stick mustache, sparse wishy-washy whiskers on a pointy chin. Cam felt like everything about him was insubstantial, a bundle of bones inside a sack of skin. Fear rippled down her spine. She'd heard this creature before.

It was . . . ?! That warlock! The one who could shape-shift into a giant lizard. The one Ileana had called Fredo. Cam remembered because at the time it had sounded to her like "a-fraid-o." He'd tried before to capture the twins. That time, their fierce protector Ileana had been there.

Now Cam was on her own.

He lunged at her, but she was too fast and too clever. Pulling a move perfected on the soccer field, Cam faked to the left, then ducked under his right arm and dashed out the door — she headed straight into the middle of the packed dance floor, which was hazy now, gradually filling with smoke.

Racing, Cam blew by shocked kids, who stopped, startled, in mid-dance.

"Get Mrs. Hammond!!" she yelled, blasting toward their principal, who was one of the chaperones.

The acrid smoke was heating up the gym. The

smoke alarms sounded. Followed by a wave of wide-spread panic.

Then, several sudden blasts nearly drowned out the hysterical crowd. Cam whirled around and saw him — Fredo! — over by the buffet! Methodically hurling meatballs up at the ceiling — with such force, he burst every lightbulb, pitching the gym into darkness!

Her own searchlight eyes could see what no one else could: The frustrated, fuming warlock turned to the stage and furiously pitched meatballs at the band. Instantly, their amplifiers sizzled and burst! What was he doing? Blowing up the gym? Cam expected to see flames shooting out from the stage.

Instead, she felt water . . . slimy, dirty, gunk-filled, rushing up to her ankles. What? Fredo was now standing against the back wall, gripping the main waterpipe with Godzilla-like strength — so hard, it burst. The smell of rotten, sewagelike slime engulfed the room. It was as if some polluted river had overflowed. The faux snow that had covered the floor now mixed with rust from the pipes.

Panic morphed to pandemonium. Marble Bay High's once enchanted evening was turning into a black and slimy nightmare; the winter wonderland now resembled a giant mosh pit, packed with frightened teenagers screaming, shoving, stampeding through the swampy floor for the doors.

The chaperones mobilized into action. Principal Hammond bounded onto the stage and grabbed the microphone from the bewildered band —

"Stay calm, everyone! Stop right now! The gym is not on fire! The flood will not hurt you. You are safe. Your teachers and chaperones will open the doors and you will file out in a calm manner."

Principal Hammond's valiant effort was no match for the rising water and the choking stench in the room. Sobbing, shrieking kids slipped and fell in swampy muck, trying to get out. Cam started to feel herself swallowed up by the crowd, caught in a tangle of swinging arms and legs. Above the din, she thought she heard her friends calling for one another. She had to do something — but what? What good was stunning people, dazzling them into confessing, and setting things afire now? The only thing she could do was see in the dark, and maybe create a beam of light that would lead people to the doorways.

But as she trained her gaze on the largest set of double doors, someone grabbed her. Shane had her by the arm. Adrenaline kicked in and with superstrength, she untangled herself and got away. That's when she saw Beth, arms flailing wildly, dress soaked, bending down — when she straightened up, Beth had pulled the much shorter Bree up off the floor, saving her from being trampled. Cam bolted over in their direction. She saw Sukari's sash, floating in the now knee-high water and felt sick, until she heard Suke's calm yet commanding voice. "Kristen! Amanda! Stay with me! Hang on!"

He grabbed her from behind. Cam felt an arm wrapped tightly around her waist. "I've got you now!"

"Never! You'll never get me!" she shrieked. Without thinking, she bent forward and sunk her teeth into his arm. It was only when he yelped, "Oww! What are you doing?" that Cam realized she hadn't foiled a warlock attacker at all, but had bitten her rescuer. Jason's arm was bleeding just above the wrist.

"Oh, no! Jason! I'm so sorry!"

"What's wrong with you? We're getting out of here!" He grabbed her, threw her over his shoulder, and bouldered out the door. To safety.

"It was him! Fredo — lizard boy!"

Hours after Cam had showered and washed her hair, her punky clone came sauntering into their room. Cam blazed through the events of the entire bizarre night at hyperspeed.

But it was Alex who accelerated in record time — from disbelief to shock to outrage. "So the creep is back — to finish what he started!"

"And this time, the scaly toad brought a friend. A hot one."

Angry at herself, Alex bit her nails, raking raw fingers through her choppy hair. "I should have been there," she kept repeating.

Instead, she'd spent most of the night in her bedroom, wrapped in one of Sara's old thin flannel shirts. Plucking at Dylan's guitar, she'd plopped herself down at Cam's computer and started composing a song, fighting to keep her mind off sleazy Isaac Fielding.

In no way was he her father. Yet he might well have a legal claim to her, one even the righteous David Barnes couldn't fight. She'd called Lucinda, who confirmed that Ike had been spotted in Crow Creek; someone had seen him at Sara's grave. Desperately, Alex had sent an e-mail to Mrs. Bass at the Crow Creek library. Maybe the librarian, a childhood friend of her mom's, could help testify or something in the upcoming hearing. Then, feeling jumpy, she'd taken a walk. The night was crisp, and it helped clear her head.

She'd been completely unprepared when she'd turned the corner onto the Barnes' block and found Cam's thoughts in her head — as if they'd been sitting on the curb, unable to travel farther, waiting for her to get there. *Where are you?* Cam was screaming telepathically. *Get your butt home! Mayday, sister!!*

Cam's sense of foreboding had been on target all along, Alex admitted to herself. They were in danger, and not just from some sneaky thief. I've been stubborn and selfish, Alex began to beat herself up, too busy wearing my outsider badge of honor to see what's going on right under my nose.

"Don't do that," Cam said, absentmindedly reading Alex's mind.

"Don't do what?"

"Don't make this about you. The introspection meter is on 'time expired.' We've got to deal. Now."

"Cam?" Alex sank into the desk chair. She was almost afraid to ask.

She didn't have to. Cam answered, "Shane so has that 'believe in me' thing going on. But was I tempted? Neh-*vuh*! Even though you weren't sending messages to me, I still heard you. You said, 'Not like this.'"

"I should have —"

"Karsh," Cam cut in. "That's who *should* have been there. He's our tracker. Our protector. He's supposed to be inside our heads, guiding us, helping us."

Alex bit her lip and said what they were both thinking, "If not him, then her."

Ileana.

Neither twin would give it a voice, but the fear was shared, and it was real. *What if Karsh or Ileana don't come? We can't fight Thantos, or the ones he sends, on our own.*

They had to make contact. By any means necessary.

In tandem, they rolled up their pj sleeves — so alike, but so different, Cam's thick, comfortable designer duds; Alex's cozy hand-me-down — and got to work. Shooing Alex off the swivel chair, Cam plunked down at the computer and started a new document. She titled it "Making Contact."

Incantations, she wrote first.

Alex, standing beside her, shook her head. "Been there, rhymed that."

"Maybe our spell reeked?" Cam ventured.

Alex shrugged. "No worse than before."

Next Cam typed: *Dad.* "We have to talk to Dad. Maybe he can get to Karsh. Besides, he knows something's up, Als. I can't read his mind, but it was written all over his face when I came home. He has a strong hunch that what happened was no accident."

Alex leaned over Cam's shoulder and backspaced *Dad.* "We can neither confirm nor deny. To involve him is to involve Emily. To ask would be to tell — everything. We can't."

Frustrated, Cam whirled in her chair. "We haven't tried hard enough!"

"Or . . ." Alex said thoughtfully, "smart enough."

"Meaning . . . ?"

"Put your sun necklace on, Cam," Alex, who was wearing her moon charm, cut in.

"Why couldn't Ileana just give us her phone number!" Cam said, walking over to her bureau and picking up the amulet. The moment she clasped it on, the familiar *ping* of an incoming IM came from the computer. It was only from Kristen. But it might as well have been a shared thought balloon over the twins' heads.

Are you thinking what I'm thinking?

E-mail!

You think Ileana has e-mail? Cam began to feel doubtful.

She is, as you would say, very circa now. Even if she's . . . not from around here, Alex thought hopefully.

But she's a witch.

"And we're not?" Alex said out loud. "Come on, Cami, put on your cyber-thinking cap. We can do this."

What would her address be? Cam tried to think.

Alex shrugged. "Shane told you where they live."

"It's a start," Cam agreed and wrote: *@coventry island.com*

Nodding, Alex added, "So, her obvious address could be: ileana@coventryisland.com."

Cam typed a quick message. Ileana, we need you! Write back now! But as soon as she pressed SEND, a

DOES NOT RECOGNIZE ADDRESS box came up. She tried *witchileana@coventryisland.com,* but that wasn't it, either.

Alex looked thoughtful. "If not a name, maybe a personality trait." Cam grinned and tried: *gogoddess.com.* When that didn't work, she typed, *imagoddessand yourenot.com.*

Cam and Alex locked eyes, identical silver-gray orbs, stormy irises outlined in inky black, and erupted in a spontaneous burst of brilliance. Had they looked out the window, they might have seen the first rays of sunlight overlaying the fast fading of the waning moon. Alex nudged Cam out of the way and typed: *callmegoddess@ coventryisland.com.*

CHAPTER FOURTEEN
SUNDAY IN SALEM

Ileana fidgeted with her hammered-gold cuff bracelet, twirling it impatiently as she waited under the imposing stone statue. Nathaniel Hawthorne! What would the famous author of *The Scarlet Letter* and *The House of Seven Gables* think if he knew he'd be immortalized for all eternity as a pigeon perch. The statue stood in the town square of his birthplace, a site famous — or rather, infamous — for another, more sinister reason.

Behind heart-shaped pink-tinted sunglasses, her smoky charcoal eyes flitted nervously. She felt almost as conspicuous as Hester Prynne. Compulsively, she drew her midnight-blue traveling cape tightly around her waist — and then, plucking at the tie and undoing it, let it billow around her.

This town always gave her the creeps. She had no idea why Brice Stanley, via an emergency e-mail, would have insisted on meeting her here. Brice was a famous Hollywood movie star and secret warlock — what possible reason would he have for being here in this ratty park? In the middle of Salem, Massachusetts?

Not that she'd dropped everything and zoomed here just because Brice asked. She was hardly some common fan, one of the millions who'd do anything for the dashing, charismatic star. She wasn't under his spell. What was that juvenile expression Apolla used? Right, she thought, kicking the grass. "Neh-vuh!"

No, Ileana had flown here for only one reason. She was desperate and didn't know where to turn. Maybe he could help her. She still hadn't figured out where Karsh was, or how to rescue her beloved, ailing mentor.

The threatening messages were becoming scarier. Be warned, Ileana, they'd said, do not dare bring the Council into this. If we find out Lady Potato, as you secretly call her, or any of the elders, has been contacted, old Karsh is as good as gone.

The last one had come only the previous night. While you waste time, he wastes away.

Then she got an IM from Brice! Had she not been so

preoccupied and panicked, she might have wondered why he was writing at this hour, predawn in California. Or why the message had sounded unlike him.

Mostly, why Salem of all places?

Well, she'd ask him as soon as he got here. Which, judging by the position of the sun and the gold pocket watch stuffed deep inside the pocket of her cape, Ileana now clocked at thirteen minutes, forty-seven seconds late. Impetuously, she pointed at the pigeon, muttered an incantation, and turned it into a chicken. As if the squawking would bring Brice there more quickly! But she had to do something: She hated tardiness — she forgave it in only one person, herself.

Crack! The tree branch snapping was at least a block away, but the brilliant witch's senses were sharp. Now she heard the unmistakable sound of tires, crunching on gravel. They were bicycle tires getting louder, rolling closer. Then the voices. Girl voices, whispers. She was about to disregard them, when she realized . . .

Ileana's cape billowed, her hair flying around her as she whirled, furious. "You two! What are you doing here?"

Astride her bike, Alex braked a couple of feet in front of Ileana and snapped off her helmet. "So you did show up." Her voice was a mix of relief and bitterness. "For him — for some movie star — you would."

Cam finished the thought. "But not for us."

Ileana's arm flew out. She had half a mind to turn the insolent twins into . . . a pair of tadpoles! But Cam ducked away swiftly. Lightning-fast, Alex caught Ileana's arm in midpose, stopping her.

She'd been tricked! How dare Apolla and Artemis be so duplicitous! It was a ruse worthy of . . . well, herself! How could they have been so clever as to *dupe* her — her! — into dropping everything and flying all the way from Coventry Island to this hated, horrible place, Salem, Massachusetts.

"We had to pick someplace we could get to on our own." Cam, who'd tossed her helmet on the ground next to her red racer, knew they'd have a ton of explaining to do. "It's a two-hour bike ride from Marble Bay."

It had taken them less time, in fact, to break into Ileana's e-mail account and figure out a plan to lure her there. Cam had started writing the urgent SOS. *We've been contacted! Lizard boy is back. You must come now!*

Alex had nixed it. "This won't work. There's a reason she's not here, a reason she never told us how to contact her."

"It's called control," Cam had snarled. "As in, she decides when she's needed. She decides when to help. She's in control."

"You'd know a thing or two about that," Alex had mocked.

Cam had ignored Alex's diss. "We've got to trick her. You're right."

That's when they began opening the e-mails in Ileana's account — and had seen the letters to and from Brice Stanley.

The movie star? Surprised, Cam had pressed her back against the chair. "She's cyber-flirting with a movie star? And he's *answering* her?"

Alex had grinned. "She's crushed on America's most self-centered . . . I mean, eligible bachelor. I bet if *he* asked to meet her, no matter how far or how soon . . ."

By eight A.M., they'd grabbed a quick breakfast, left a note for Dave and Emily, mounted their bikes, and were off. Cam knew the way: She'd been on two class trips to historic Salem and had felt creepy there both times. Now, she knew why. The witch trials had been held there in the seventeenth century. Maybe one of their ancestors had been put to death there.

The twins had pulled an all-nighter, yet now as Alex earnestly explained why they needed her help, Cam couldn't help thinking it was Ileana who looked exhausted. She was pale, her hair had lost its golden luster, and bordered on unkempt.

Alex picked up Cam's train of thought, telepathically adding, *She's lost too much weight.*

Cam scanned Ileana's outfit, what she could see beneath the cape. Her capris needed ironing. . . .

"If you lured me here to play beauty and fashion police, I'll turn you into Joan and Melissa Rivers," Ileana snapped, reading their minds.

"What's with the depress-o-rama?" Alex said softly. "Haven't you heard a single word I've said? It's lizard boy, the sequel: Fredo's on the scene, and he's trying to get us. It's an emergency!"

"Aren't they all!" Ileana seemed unmoved.

Gently, Cam touched her shoulder. "Sorry we tricked you. We tried incantations, but you didn't hear us. We're in trouble."

Ileana shrunk from Cam's touch and snapped, "Take a number!"

"We get to cut the line," Alex retorted. "Our needs come before yours. . . ."

Ileana threw her head back and laughed bitterly. "My needs? As if that's why I haven't dropped everything and come to your aid."

"So you heard us — ?" Cam was puzzled.

"— And deliberately didn't come?" Alex was hurt.

"Smart little T*Witches! Now you've got it! You snap your fingers, I don't jump. So you resort to trickery. Too bad you've wasted your time." She stopped midrant. "How did you know my password?"

"We didn't," Cam explained. "It took us all night, trying to think of everything we knew about you. We thought you might use a name. Someone close to you."

"Karsh."

Ileana turned away so they wouldn't see her lip tremble. "The magic word."

Cam saw it before Alex heard it. The icy chill whirled around her, goose bumps rose on her arms, and the throbbing in her temples began. Her eyes stung. But she saw: a room so small and sloped, a tall person had to stoop in certain places. A room so enclosed, only a few people could be in it at the same time, so dark you needed a flashlight. Or a candle.

Then Alex heard it: the creaking of wooden steps, or was it fragile bones? Background noises she couldn't identify, but if she had to pin them, they sounded like a lion's roar, and then a goat's neigh, and faintest of all, a raspy whisper.

Together, Cam and Alex exclaimed, "Karsh is in trouble!"

Astoundingly, Ileana burst into tears. But only for a second. Wiping her gold-flecked eyes with the back of her hand, she admitted, sniffing, "They've got him, and I don't know where he is."

Cam felt her throat constrict. "Who . . . who's got him?"

Ileana's words pierced her heart. "Who do you think?"

Tremulously, Alex said, "Thantos? He's got the power to kidnap Karsh?"

"Fredo, the idiot uncle, is there, too," Ileana spat bitterly.

Cam was confused. "Uncle? Thantos is our father's brother, right? Where does —"

"Who said Aron had only one brother?"

Alex felt her stomach turn to jelly. Cam trembled.

Ileana had forgotten how much the twins didn't know. She felt exhausted suddenly and was grateful the statue had a base. She sank down onto it, and told the twins some — but hardly all — of their family history. How the brothers had grown up on Coventry Island. How Karsh, who'd mentored Aron, had grown closest to the brilliant and kind warlock.

Cam found the words they both wanted to ask. "And our mother. You knew —"

Ileana took a deep breath. How much would Lord Karsh want her to say? At the thought of him, tears welled up again. Pressing her lips together, she said, "Miranda is gone. Vanished soon after you were born."

Alex whispered, "Is she dead?"

"No one has seen her in fifteen years, so it's assumed," Ileana said. "Only —"

"Only what?" Cam jumped in anxiously.

"Nothing."

"Not nothing!" Alex gripped her arm.

"They never found" — *a body,* Ileana wanted to say, but instead said — "proof of her death."

A soft breeze could have knocked Alex and Cam over. Instead, a furious biting wind rose up from the east — from the water. Alex's head was spinning. She couldn't think of any way to stop it, except this: "Karsh! We'll find him," she blurted. "We'll help you find him."

"There's nothing more important than that!" Cam knew she sounded over-the-top. She felt like her blood was boiling, veins and arteries pulsing hard against her skin.

"We can help, let us," Cam pleaded, then described the room she'd seen, yelling over Alex's shouts of the sounds she'd just heard when thinking of Karsh.

Ileana thought, So earnest! And fierce! She'd just divulged a family secret that shook them to the core. And yet, finding Karsh was uppermost in their minds. When it came to helping someone else, Apolla and Artemis had no fear and knew no bounds.

Ileana could not accept their help. The girls were Thantos's quarry. He'd do anything to get them.

Not on her watch.

So she dismissed their anxious pleas to help.

"Here's the equation," she told them. "You help me, they win. They *want* both Karsh and me out of the way, so you are left unprotected."

"If that's true," Cam reminded Ileana, "they're already winning."

"Give me a break, I'm working on it!" Exasperated, Ileana sprang up and began to pace, circling the statue. "I'll figure it out on my own!"

Alex recognized the look on Ileana's face. The brave and beautiful witch was fighting not to let her terror show. Alex's heart went out to her. There must be *something* she could do.

As if wishing could make it so, a bolt of inspiration charged through her like electricity racing through a circuit. There was a way to help. She asked her distraught witch-guardian, "Do you have any herbs on you?"

Startled, Ileana blurted, "Of course! I always carry monkshood, parsley, and sage. He needs these to make the potions!"

Cam realized Ileana was talking about Karsh. And she locked into her twin's vibe instantly. Holding her palm out, she stepped toward Ileana. "Can I look at them?"

Ileana impatiently peeled off the pouch slung over her shoulder. She tossed it at Cam with a look that said, *As if you would know what to do with these!*

Alex quickly unclasped her necklace while communicating to Cam, *Give me your sun necklace now!* A second later, the gold amulets lay on Alex's open, outstretched palm, intertwined.

Meanwhile, Cam had opened the pouch and sprinkled the herbs, which Ileana had already ground into a fine powder, on her own open palm.

They needed an incantation, now! But which one?

Of course, Cam thought — a healing one. Alex began, and she chimed in.

Universe of love and health,
Use these gifts of nature's wealth
To free Ileana from the doubt that renders her undone, grant her power to win this bout
With moon magick and curing sun.

Alex felt the tingling first, then the necklaces heating up, accompanied by a faint buzzing sound. The magick was working; the sun and the moon charms were fusing together!

Although Ileana had witnessed this before, the sheer power of Aron's twin daughters acting as one left her awestruck.

Alex hadn't planned what she was going to do next. She felt Cam's hand squeeze her shoulder and closed her eyes and forced herself to envision the necklaces — the amulets meant to protect her and Cam. Ileana needed the gold sun-moon charms, but would never take them. Could Alex give them to her guardian some other way?

A sudden anger overtook her, a rage against the monsters who'd taken Karsh captive. Fueled by her venom, Alex saw them floating up from her palm, into the air, and settling in the deep velvety pocket of Ileana's cape.

When she opened her eyes, her palm was empty.

Ileana shivered. Now the twins were completely unprotected.

CHAPTER FIFTEEN
SEEING IS DECEIVING

"Are you sure you did the right thing?" Cam asked anxiously as the twins trekked back to Marble Bay.

"I'm not sure of anything," Alex answered, trying not to sound defensive. "Except this: Ileana needs help. What else do I need to be sure of?"

Cam frowned. "Our parents made them for us. . . ."

Alex closed her mind. Mention of their parents would lead to Miranda. If she was alive, she'd abandoned them. If she wasn't . . . Alex pushed down hard on the black rubber pedals of the mountain bike and pulled ahead of her twin.

Cam quickly caught up. "I want to help Ileana, too. But she's not the only one in trouble. So are we — that's why we tricked her into meeting us. You just gave her the only defense we have. The necklaces might not even work for her."

The late autumn day, bright with biting sunshine that morning, had turned overcast. Alex slowed down. "She could be related to us."

"Her eyes are the same as ours," Cam admitted, adding, "and the branches of this family tree are one tangled mess. . . ."

"Whoever she is," Alex concluded, "she can't help us now. We have to deal on our own."

And they did.

To keep their mind off Karsh and Ileana, Cam and Alex spent every spare minute of the next two days plotting how to smash the web of deceit that had caught Beth — and could trap them.

They started early Monday morning before school, digging into the organization called Helping Hands. Was it legit? Cam went on-line, but the website was identical to the pamphlets at the mall. They were full of hype, cleverly appealing to people with a soft spot for the helpless, and who were willing to work on their behalf. It didn't tell them anything they didn't already know.

Cam was about to hit EXIT when Alex stopped her.

"Hang on. Forget about what's there. Think about what's missing."

"Huh?" Cam scrunched her forehead.

"There's a ton of info about why they're raising money, the services they provide to children, but no specific mention of where the money's going."

Cam shrugged. "We know where it's going — Sunshine House."

"And that piece of crucial info would be missing from the website . . . why?"

"Because . . . there's no such place?" Cam guessed.

She was wrong. Sunshine House was real, all right. The info on its website confirmed what Helping Hands had described, a professionally staffed shelter for abused and abandoned children. A safe place for kids to be until they could either go home or into foster care, it was located in California, just south of Los Angeles.

"How convenient," snorted Alex. "Beth Fish, of Marble Bay, Massachusetts, can't exactly drop by and see her hard-raised funds at work."

Cam considered. "Ms. Webb told Beth that Helping Hands actually runs the shelter. Even if that's an exaggeration, they've got to be a major benefactor."

If they're on the level.

"So how do we find out?" Alex said.

"I'm sure there's some kind of law that says a not-for-profit place has to divulge where the Benji's are coming from. My dad would know."

"But we're not involving him, remember? Besides, why would they divulge *anything* to a pair of nosy fifteen-year-olds?" Alex noted.

"Who said anything about two teenagers asking?" Cam's eyes twinkled. She expertly set up a new screen name on her e-mail account.

A slow grin spread across Alex's face. She edged Cam out of the way to begin the letter.

Dear Sunshine House,

I've heard about the excellent work you do on behalf of unfortunate children. I'd like to help out. But my advisors — you know how they are! — insist I find out more about the funding you already receive before I make my donation. Could you send me a complete list of your benefactors? I'm sure you understand the need for complete secrecy. Please respond to this e-mail address, which in no way identifies me, but which I've set up specifically for this fact-finding purpose.

Cam elbowed Alex out of the way and finished it, Respectfully yours, Brice Stanley.

Alex hit SEND MAIL.

*   *   *

At Marble Bay High, the debacle at the dance was topic A. Miraculously, and thanks to the quick action of the chaperones and local police, no one had been seriously hurt.

What had gone wrong in the gym? How could the wiring *and* the plumbing have gone kerbloohey at the same moment? It had to be sabotage, went the prevailing opinion. All students who'd eyewitnessed the disaster were required to talk with the authorities. But the perpetrator and the motive remained elusive. Was it a kid with a grudge? A rival school's sports team? A random psycho?

Only three beings knew. And they would never tell.

Meanwhile, the gymnasium would be in rehab for several weeks, so all PE classes were either held outdoors or canceled outright. The school had also set up special guidance sessions for anyone who felt traumatized by Saturday night's disaster.

Of the Six Pack, Brianna seemed most affected by the experience. Beth had saved her from getting trampled. Because she simply couldn't say "thank you" in her Bree-way, she was making an effort to become closer to Beth. Cam squashed the pang of jealousy she felt seeing them walk down the hall together giggling, passing notes in class, and sharing the sushi Bree had delivered to the cafeteria. *Beth is* my *best friend — Bree barely used to tolerate her. . . .*

Eyes on the prize, was the telepathic message from Alex. *What we're doing for Beth is what's important.*

Their investigation took a giant leap forward when Cam and Alex got home from school. Logging on, the happy sound of "you've got mail" greeted them.

Dear Mr. Stanley,

Thank you for your recent inquiry. We would be honored to count you among our supporters. In the enclosed attachment, you will find information about our facility and the children we serve. Included is the list you requested.

It was signed Oliver O'Day, director, Sunshine House.

Cam held her breath as Alex clicked on the attachment. The shelter received funding from no less than 150 divergent sources, organizations, and individuals. All were listed alphabetically.

Helping Hands, which should have been between Have-A-Heart and Just For Kids, was not there.

"So it's official," Cam declared. "Our hunch was right; Helping Hands is a huge scam-o-rama." She picked up the phone.

"Who are you calling?" Alex demanded.

"Beth! And then Mrs. Hammond — and hello, my dad!"

"Down, girl. Jumping to conclusions is not one of the events in this competition," Alex advised. "There still could be some logical reason why it's not listed among the donors. All we know for sure is: Helping Hands doesn't 'run' or probably even support Sunshine House, and neither Ms. Webb nor Shane is what they pretend to be. But," Alex cautioned, "twin lies don't build a truth. *We* need to build our case."

Cam was impressed with Alex's careful logic. It was a side of her sis rarely on display. She had to laugh. "You sound like a lawyer's daughter. I thought that was my position in this household."

"In case you didn't notice" — Alex's lip curled mischievously — "there's been a little shifting of positions in the home game of Barnes Family Dysfunction since I got there."

Impulsively, Cam hugged her. "Lucky for all of us."

"Yo, we're gonna need more than luck to unravel this mystery," Alex reminded her, squiggling out of Cam's embrace. "On to stage two, sista."

CHAPTER SIXTEEN
BREAKING THROUGH

The law firm of Crunkle, Wong, Barnes, and DiBenedico was located in the business section of Marble Bay. The offices were in a three-story Revolutionary-war-era townhouse that the partners had bought a decade ago. Cam had always loved going there. The dark wood-paneled walls lined with bookshelves, the winding stairway, the rich aroma of coffee brewing, had seemed inviting and cozy to her. Everyone was friendly to her — she was the boss's daughter. Of course, she'd never been there when it was dark and deserted.

Until now.

She and Alex, using the excuse of an emergency library excursion, had jumped on their bikes after dinner and pedaled the two and a half miles to the office. Cam was nervous, but she didn't feel guilty about breaking into Dave's office. How weird was that?

Reading her mind, Alex responded, "Because you're doing something righteous. And besides, you're not technically breaking in. You have the keys."

"Correction: I stole the —"

"Override: borrowed," Alex reminded her as they parked their bikes and walked up the three steps to the front door. "You're only borrowing them for an hour or so. As soon as we get home, if you can't sneak them back into his desk drawer, I'll use a little magic and replace them."

"Show-off," Cam muttered. "Make yourself useful — use your hyperhearing for any random sounds while I open the locks." After turning the several locks, Cam waited for the low buzz of the alarm. Expertly, she hit the right numbers to disengage it.

Alex was impressed. It hadn't occurred to her that there would be an alarm — or that Cam would know the code. "Dave must really trust you."

"Maybe he knew I'd need it someday. And trusted that if I used it without telling him, it would be for a good reason."

"It is, Cami. It is. Come on, let's do this."

What Cam didn't have was the slightest idea of

where to find what they were looking for: the file for the Lizzie Andrews case. "Remember," she cautioned Alex, "all we want is her address, so we can talk to her. No excess snooping."

"So if I happen to find something related to the Barnes vs. Fielding hearing — your family against icky Ike — I shouldn't even look at it, right?"

Cam heaved a sigh. There was no answer to that one.

Or to the more immediate problem: The file cabinets in Dave's third-floor office were locked. A situation Cam hadn't counted on. Of course, she didn't have the keys. What power could she use now? She couldn't exactly melt the locks.

Alex read her mind. *How 'bout the power of common sense? Where does Dave —*

"Got it!" Cam understood. Her dad would likely keep the keys to the files in a place similar to where he kept the office keys in the house. She checked his desk drawer. Left side.

Ignoring her own vow not to eyeball anything confidential, Cam read through the entire file. Lizzie Andrews, a fifteen-year-old foster child living in Waverly, Massachusetts, the next town over, had been caught stealing a pair of diamond earrings from a store in Boston by a security camera. She'd been working with an adult accomplice, who got away — and who she has refused to identify. The salesperson had given a description of the woman: tall, thin, blond hair, brown eyes. She could have been almost anyone.

Cam jotted down Lizzie's address, then carefully replaced the file, exactly where it had been.

Alex, meanwhile, had her nose in a different file. Like Cam, she'd found what she was looking for.

Cutting class was not something Cam ordinarily did, but she purposely chose the middle of the afternoon on the next day to pay Lizzie a visit. It was her best shot at finding the girl alone. From the file, she'd learned Lizzie's foster parents worked, and until her trial date, she was being home-schooled by a tutor who might be gone by the time Cam got there.

So just before her last class, Cam sneaked out of school and walked to the bus stop for the half-hour ride to Waverly. She went alone, because, following their plan, Alex had something of equal importance to do.

The address Cam had copied down belonged to a small brick row house. Her stomach a tangle of knots, Cam walked up two steps to the front door and rang the bell.

"If you're selling something, we're not buying." The woman who answered the door was so large, she filled the frame.

"D-does Lizzie Andrews live here?" Cam stammered.

"Who wants to know?"

"A . . . friend . . . ?" Cam tried. "I mean, from school." She smiled hopefully. "I have a book to give her."

The woman looked Cam up and down, then apparently decided she wasn't a threat and summoned Lizzie to the door. "You've got five minutes," she said, and walked away.

If it was possible, the girl Cam remembered was even paler, more fidgety and beaten down than she had been that day at the mall. Dark purple circles ringed her eyes, evidence of wakeful nights.

She recognized Cam immediately. Her hand flew to her mouth; her eyes popped. But before she could scream — or slam the door — Cam assured her, "I'm not here to hurt you, Lizzie. I'm here to help."

Lizzie let her guard down for a moment. "What are you doing here? What do you want?" she whispered nervously.

"Is there somewhere we could talk?" Cam scanned the dimly lit room behind the girl.

Over her shoulder, Lizzie called to the woman

who'd answered the door, "Rose? I'm sitting outside for a minute. I'll be right in."

The answer came back, "Keep the door open. So I can see you."

"Is that your foster mom?" Cam asked as Lizzie guardedly sat down next to her.

The nervous girl's jaw tightened. "No. She's my court-appointed watchdog — wait, how do you even know I have a foster mother? Who are you?"

Cam took a deep breath. "My bad. Rewind: I'm Cam. Barnes."

"Barnes? You mean . . . you're related to —"

Cam shrugged. "Six-degree world, huh? He's my dad."

Lizzie paled. "So obviously you told him about . . . that day at the mall."

"I didn't, actually," Cam said, and saw Lizzie relax. "It wasn't my place to — but things have changed. I really need you to tell me the whole story."

She shook her head. "I can't."

"Maybe if you knew why —" Before the girl could protest, Cam told Lizzie about Ms. Webb showing up as her substitute. And about Beth, who trusted the shifty woman and was working for Helping Hands. Beth, whose grades were plummeting, who was involved with a guy up to no good. Cam talked about her fear that Beth might soon be lured into stealing, as Lizzie had.

Lizzie's question took Cam by surprise. "Your friend Beth? Is she . . . a foster child?"

"No! She lives with her bio-folks, the whole nuclear family thing. Why do you ask?"

"Forget it." Lizzie shrugged and started to stand up. "So if you can ID Webb, why do you need me?"

Because I can't tell anyone what I know, Cam thought. Because if I did, everyone would find out I'm a witch. Who can do things . . . well, like this:

She and Alex had composed an incantation the night before. Which Cam would use only if she had to. Before Lizzie could turn away, Cam trained her magnetic eyes on the frightened girl and chanted,

"Your burden is too heavy, your shoulders slim and frail,

It's your secrets that enslave you, your shame that makes you fail.

Free yourself, Lizzie Andrews, from the chains that bind you.

Trust in me and tell me all; freedom and peace will find you. . . ."

Cam bit her lip at that last line, hoping . . . hoping . . .

Lizzie's eyes glazed over. And she told her story.

Many hours later, sitting next to Cam at Dave's office, she repeated it. Trusting father and daughter, Lizzie confessed that she'd been lured into the shoplifting ring through the ruse of Helping Hands. That she'd been warned — if she ever told the truth, Webb would get her booted right out of her foster home. "They prey on kids who come from broken homes," Lizzie tearfully told them.

Cam's heart broke for this girl as Dave gently asked the big question: "Do you know where the money's really going?"

"Not to help kids. I didn't know that then, but now I do — it's going right into the pockets of Cecilia Webb and her little ring of slimy thieves."

By the time Lizzie had finished, she'd given details not only about the robbery she'd been caught at, but the ones before, those she'd gotten away with.

Cam's emotions matched Lizzie's. Relief and anxiety washed over her — mixed with a dash of guilt. So far, David Barnes hadn't asked his daughter how she'd come to talk to Lizzie Andrews, how she'd brought his client to his office and convinced her to open up. Cam didn't have any truthful answers to give him. She hoped he'd just go with it, trust her. Cam needed to tell Dave one more thing. She hoped he wouldn't ask how she knew. "Dad, tell the police to check Webb's cell phone calls. I think there's someone in prison she's been calling."

An hour later, Dave had contacted the police and a warrant had been issued for the arrest of Cecilia Webb — who Lizzie told him also went by the name of Belinda Rogers. Cam flashed on the receipt in the car: So that's what BR stood for. Lizzie explained that the woman made frequent trips to Boston to pick up the fake jewelry they used to make the switches.

Trompe l'oeil — a "trick of the eye," as Dave had explained the store's name. How appropriate, Cam thought.

Cam gave herself major props. All by herself, she'd found a way to free poor Lizzie and bring that shady woman down.

Too much time would pass before she found out how premature her back-patting was.

CHAPTER SEVENTEEN
SWITCHING SISTERS

All Cam's friends, including Beth, knew about the afternoon's "switch-a-ruse." Alex was going to try and pass as her twin in social studies class. The Six Pack didn't know why. They didn't ask. But Brianna, Beth, Kristen, Sukari, and Amanda wouldn't have been fooled anyway — not by a baseball cap and wearing Cam's makeup and Gap clothes, which felt stiff and starchy to Alex.

Ms. Webb was Alex's target. She needed to get close enough, for long enough, to break into the woman's head. It had been three days since the disaster at the dance, and Cam had said Webb seemed different that Monday, shaken up. Was the woman shaky enough to be thinking out loud?

Alex was in luck. Only not exactly the kind she was hoping for.

If Webb realized it was not Cam, but Alex, sitting in the third row, her hair hidden beneath a Boston Red Sox cap, she gave no indication of it. Her teaching style, as Cam had warned, was brusque, intimidating if you weren't used to it, and unforgiving. Not that Alex had trouble with the work. Cam had coached her, and she was a quick study.

As it turned out, breaking into Webb's head wasn't all that hard. But it also wasn't all that informative. For most of the period, her mind really was on the lesson. Snooze-inducing as it was.

When Webb's wily thoughts turned to the class, she practically sniveled, *Look at them with their fruit-fly attention spans.* Of Scott Marino, she thought, *Am I glad that little blindness act was temporary! The last thing I need is attention focused on me.* Then she focused on Brianna. *Spoiled little brat. Yet she knows her stuff, I have to give her that.*

Webb's steely gaze shifted to Beth Fish: *There's my star pupil! At the big event, that's when we turn her into a real fund-raiser!*

The event? What? Where? When? Alex wasn't sure what that meant. Only that something big was going down.

Then Webb turned to Alex. *Little Miss Barnes,* she mistakenly thought, *acting like she's got something on me. If she did, she'd have sprung it already. They can't prove a thing. The nerve of those delinquent twins messing up the Jewelry Corner heist. The only thing going down around here are Miss Barnes's grades.*

So when the eraser leaped out of Webb's hand, leaving a trail of dust all over her shiny black blouse, when the book flew off Brianna's desk and swiped the substitute, bruising her arm, and when she tripped over Scott Marino's backpack, which suddenly tumbled into the aisle, could Alex be blamed? Nuh-*uh*!

At the bell, Alex sprang out of her seat. She was halfway to the door when she felt a tap on her shoulder. Brianna. Too loudly, little miss wordplay teased, "Where are you going, Cami-*mole*?"

Alex shrugged. "Home."

Bree lowered her voice. "We're all going to PITS. Might as well go all the way, Cam-for-a-day."

Alex removed her cap and pulled the Cam-scrunchie out of her hair. "I don't think so."

"Yet, I do," Bree cajoled. "Unless Cam's coming back. From wherever she really is. . . ."

Bree was digging for dish. Alex decided to not give it to her.

*   *   *

An hour later, the Six Pack settled into their booth at Pie In The Sky — or PITS — with their usual two-pizza, six-drink order on the table in front of them. The disaster at the dance seemed forgotten, the mood was up-beat, and the chatter, to Alex, inane. Topics: boys, soccer, grades, soccer . . . blah, blah, blah. Alex tuned out, hoping Cam would show — she was anxious to find out what happened with Lizzie.

"We've raised a thousand dollars so far, and that's in only two weeks." *That* got Alex's attention. Beth was talking, waving her hands excitedly. "Two pretty intense weeks!"

"You personally?" Bree asked, carefully carving off the crust from her slice of pizza.

Beth giggled. "Well, not to toot my own horn, but Shane and I designed these awesome flyers, we mailed bunches out, stuck others on car windshields. And I talked to store owners, got donations, you know."

"You toot, girl!" Amanda said. "That's so awesome, but —" She stopped, unsure of how to phrase what she wanted to say next.

Kristen had no problem saying it for her. "Maybe if you put some of that selfless time back into homework . . ."

"Sore-topic alert," Sukari cautioned. "But on the

real, Fish, you tanked on the science test. And that's your best subject."

"Maybe what's real for me right now" — Beth should have sounded defensive, but there was sadness in her voice — "is helping the helpless, not being selfish."

Kristen's dark eyes flashed. "Oh, like because I care about my grades that makes me selfish?"

Amanda broke in, "Of course she doesn't think that! She's just following a kind of path right now, but she'll get her balance back."

Beth looked hurt, so Amanda added, "Anyway, I want to hear more about what you're doing for the kids — are you sending them books and toys and stuff?"

"We're sending them money to buy books. And clothes. The money we've raised is really going to help." *And we'll more than double that after the event!*

"What ev — ?" The words popped from Alex's mouth before she realized Beth hadn't said that out loud. Luckily, Kristen and Bree were on to a sidebar convo and no one had heard Alex.

So she continued to plug into Beth's brain. *If I could only tell them about the rave! The Rave to Save, such a cool name that Ms. Webb made up. We're going to raise a ton more money!*

The rave? Was that the event Webb had been thinking about? Alex drummed her fingers on the table. A rave — well, where she came from, anyway — was dangerous. Dark, loud, crowded, and sometimes a place where illegal, bad things went on. But maybe it was different here, on planet Cutesy-ville. But if Webb were involved . . .

I just wish I knew when the rave was, in case I have to buy something. Shane said he'd call as soon as he knows. I'm not sure what to wear. Usually, I'd ask Cam — like that's about to happen!

Alex jumped up and tapped Beth's arm. "I need to talk to you — in private?"

Beth was puzzled. But Alex heard her thinking, *Hmmm . . . maybe Alex is interested in Helping Hands. She's not her sister.* So Alex knew that Beth was truly blindsided when, in the ladies' room, she blurted, "It's about Shane. What do you even know about him?"

Beth's shoulders slumped. "Shane? What do you care? You sound more like your sister every day."

"Is that a bad thing, Beth?"

"These days, it isn't great."

Alex persisted, "Do you know how old he is? Where he lives? Where he goes to school? What his *agenda* is?"

Defensive, Beth said, "I know what I need to know. And right now, I know I need to get back to the table."

She turned away and walked out the door. But not

before Alex heard one final thought. It surprised and saddened her. *What is up with Cam and Alex? Why can't they see? Shane and Helping Hands are the only good things in my life. My parents don't stop fighting. My mom cries all the time. My dad won't talk, he doesn't want to tell me, I think he's moving out. I can't . . . I don't . . . I won't . . . think about it.*

CHAPTER EIGHTEEN
A BIRD IN HAND

A small, gabled, wood-framed cottage sat on a tiny plot of land at the end of a block. Except for the fresh coat of white paint it got every so often, it was preserved pretty much intact from the time it was built, many centuries ago. The house was like many others in town. It stood out in no way. Which was one reason Lord Thantos had wanted it, the minute he'd seen it. And what Thantos wanted, he got.

The interior was again ordinary, except for one unusual feature. Inside a hall closet, a trapdoor opened to a secret staircase.

The wooden steps, worn with age, led down to a

small room. The only light came from two tiny, basementlike windows. A musty, mildewed scent permeated the damp stone room, as if it hadn't been inhabited in many years. Long ago, it had served a righteous purpose. It had sheltered some who were accused of witchcraft and would have been put to death if discovered. But that was then.

To Karsh, it was a dungeon. Would it be his last resting place?

Rest? He almost laughed. At least his captors had unbound him. Rope and chains were no longer needed — he was too weak to flee. Thantos was allowing just enough food to keep him alive. Use of magick might temporarily ease the hunger pains. Like all of their kind, Karsh was human, and eventually, he would succumb to starvation.

Until then, he had his pain to remind him he was very much alive! The arthritis that caused his ankles to ache every time he stood, or worse, tried to walk. Spasms of shooting pain attacked his back, and it was getting harder to keep his hands from trembling. He needed his tonics, his homemade potions and elixirs to keep his symptoms under control and his suffering at bay.

Still, his mind was as sharp as ever. Karsh knew well where he was, but steadfastly refused to form the name of the place in his brain. Ileana could contact him tele-pathically. If his only victory was to keep her from falling into this trap, it would be worth his death.

He leveled a glance at his kidnappers. Fredo, drool-ing as his head slumped on his bony shoulder, asleep in the chair. Thantos stood by the window, expectantly. It was taking longer than it should have, the merciless brute was thinking. The mercurial witch had shown tremendous strength of will. But time was not on her side. It wouldn't be long. Ileana would not let the suffer-ing continue.

"You of all people" — unexpectedly, Karsh re-minded Thantos that he could still tap into unuttered thoughts — "should not underestimate Ileana."

Thantos whirled and trained heavy-lidded eyes on his captive. "What I don't underestimate — though I will never understand it — is her devotion to you. She will come. Bank on it. In fact, I'd say your life depends on it."

"Ileana," Karsh rasped, "will do what she must to protect your brother's daughters. She is too smart to fall for your ploy. She won't come, Thantos."

"Too smart, is she? Her head may tell her one thing, but she will follow her heart. Straight here."

"Never," Karsh repeated.

Thantos shrugged. "Then I guess we'll have to up the ante." He pulled out a vial from his vest pocket and waved it in front of Karsh's watery eyes. "I had this made specially for you. I'll tell you what's in it. A lively mix of the rootstock and leaves of monkshood, a pinch of sage leaves, and parsley seeds. When blended in just the right way, they form the basis for a certain elixir — just the kind, I believe, that you use to free yourself from constant, debilitating pain. Want to see?"

Karsh tried but couldn't keep himself from hungering after it. Just a few drops, if he could only sip a few drops, he could get some of his strength back, strength he desperately needed. Ileana wasn't ready. And the girls were mere fledglings. He'd never failed a fledgling before.

"There's a first time for everything, my old friend. Failure, too." Meanly, Thantos turned the tube upside down, watching in mock horror as the green-gold liquid pooled on the stone floor. "Ooops, I spilled it . . . again."

The flapping of bird wings startled him. Karsh had dozed but was now suddenly wide awake. He knew what that sound meant. No, his heart cried! Against all of his prayers, Ileana had come.

Ileana had never left Salem. She'd meant to, especially after Apolla and Arte — that is, Camryn and Alexandra — pedaled away on bicycles they one day would no longer need. After their initiation, when they were sixteen, they would have many more efficient and interesting ways to travel.

Ileana didn't know exactly what had made her stay rooted to the spot. She was compelled to follow her instincts. They were all she had right now.

Correction: as she fumbled in her pocket, she felt the twins' necklaces. Alexandra had been well intentioned — such a pure girl! — but Ileana doubted they could really help her. *Free Ileana from self-doubt.* She laughed. One day, she would teach the twins to compose real incantations. Yet somehow, she did feel surer of herself. Stronger.

She'd walked east from Salem Common to the water, and she sat by a pier on Derby Wharf. Groups of tourists passed, on their way to the famous historic sites.

She hadn't meant to tune into the tour guide's spiel: "During the witchcraft trials in 1692, the accusations of a group of children and women caused nineteen people to be hanged. Come see a reenactment as the innocent victims come alive and plead to a deaf justice system caught up in the hysteria of the time."

Ileana wasn't interested in their revisionist history. She might not have known her own personal history — she'd been orphaned as an infant and Karsh had raised her — but she knew enough about this place.

Karsh used to tell her. Of the dark time when anyone who was even thought to be different in some way was persecuted. His own grandmother —

A brilliant and beautiful woman, too smart for her time. A doctor she'd be now, Karsh told Ileana, *but back then —! She was put to death for healing others.*

Ileana could hear his raspy voice in her head.

Wait! That *was* his raspy voice! Ileana jerked up. She scanned the block of houses to her left. She felt nothing. She trained her sparkling eyes on the block to her right and honed in on the house on the end, an old gabled cottage, which boasted nothing modern except paint.

She flew in through the window. First, she hovered above the sleeping Fredo's head. She chirped gaily as he jumped out of his chair, frantically trying to wipe the droppings off his head — a little gift Ileana couldn't restrain herself from giving.

Instantly, Thantos realized what happened.

The villainous warlock mocked her. "A pigeon? A common pigeon? My dear Ileana, I'd have thought you more imaginative. If you were going to shape-shift into a bird to fly through our little window, why not an eagle? Or at the very least —"

"A crow?" she responded sarcastically.

"Precisely," Thantos mused. "Although apparently I'm the one with something to crow about."

She zoomed straight for Thantos, flew right into his craggy face, and flapped her wings madly. Just as his muscled arm flung out to swipe her, she zipped away. Ileana settled at Karsh's feet and said, "It's over, I'm here now."

Use of her real voice confused the still-fouled Fredo. It wasn't until the short pigeon legs elongated, the wings folded in and became arms, the convex chest morphed into a woman's torso, and the small bird head reformed into Ileana's exquisite face, did he understand. And became so enraged Thantos banished him from the room.

Ileana knew she'd find Karsh in bad shape, but she couldn't help the gasp that escaped her lips. With a stab of pain, she realized what the kidnapping had cost him. His pallor was gray, his frame skeletal, the creases that defined his weathered face had deepened. But his eyes were alive.

"What did you think you could do in that shape?" Thantos was taunting. "Or were you planning to use pigeon droppings to free him? Or flap him free?"

Ileana ignored Thantos. "Lord Karsh." She bowed before her mentor. "I'm so sorry. It's my fault —"

In a voice barely above a whisper, Karsh reassured

her, "Guilt is not a productive emotion, my child. Use it only to learn a lesson, then discard it."

"Good advice, Ileana. You shouldn't feel guilty about allowing my brother to escape. Which led to Lord Karsh's kidnapping. And your paltry attempt at rescue." Thantos gathered up the thick rope and chains from the corner he'd tossed them in after untying Karsh.

Ileana hung her head. She'd acted impulsively, wanting only to get to Karsh in the quickest way possible. She had no plan for freeing him. Once again, she realized as Thantos now used the ropes to bind her wrists to Karsh's, her impatience was her downfall. She was in danger of not only failing Karsh, but truly abandoning the twins, who'd come to her for help.

Barging in on her thoughts, Thantos cackled, "Yes, my nieces do seem to be in quite the pickle right now. Without the protection you seem unable to provide right now, Artemis and Apolla are easy prey."

Karsh tried to quash what he knew would be an Ileana explosion. To no avail. She lashed out, "Don't underestimate them. Together they can foil you!"

"How unfortunate for them, then," Thantos said menacingly, "that at the appointed time, they won't be together."

CHAPTER NINETEEN
THE TIME HAS COME

Cam couldn't sleep. Her mind hummed like a motor she couldn't shut off, yet she couldn't concentrate on anything for longer than a flicker of a moment. Not her homework, not the book she'd been reading, Jane Austen's *Emma*, not even the magazines that usually distracted her. They lay unread at the side of her bed, beneath the CDs and headphones. Even in the dark, the piece playing in her head would not be quieted.

She should have been psyched. Her hunch about Lizzie had totally paid off. All by herself, she'd given the trusting girl a way to do what she really wanted: confess. Cam had helped free the trapped teen from Webb's blackmail *and* from guilt. And isn't that what her powers were for? For extra credit, she'd managed to stop Webb from ever snaring another vulnerable kid.

It was in the bonus round she'd blown it. In what had been most important in her whole entire life: her friendship with Beth. Cam's hunches, her foresight, her stun-gun eyesight had led a total stranger to the light, but when it came to Beth, she herself had been blind.

Cam had not been able to see what was in front of her all the time. There was a reason Beth had fallen so easily into Webb's trap and into trusting Shane. The good-natured ever-steady friend been emotionally off-balance, freaked about her parents. Beth had tried to tell her, but Cam wasn't listening. Ears and eyes closed. Some friend.

As soon as Alex downloaded her, she'd jumped to the phone — every instinct had been to call Beth and "make it right," but Alex had stopped her. "It's not like she told me; I read her mind. Besides, if you call now, it'll be so you can feel better. It won't be for her."

"So color me selfish," Cam had said glumly. "Everyone else does."

Alex mimed playing the violin. "Poor little Cami. Everyone thinks she's so self-serving — when she's so not!" At Cam's grimace, Alex reminded her, "What you've already done will help Beth more than anything —"

"And what we will do — surgery to remove Shane from her life," Cam had finished the thought.

Als was right. Tomorrow was another day. After what she'd accomplished today, Beth was safe from Webb and "Helping Scams" forever. There'd be no more meetings, no more fund-raising — Cam made a mental note to tell her dad about Mrs. Fish's missing necklace, sure now that Beth had "donated it." After today, there would certainly be no event, no rave.

Tomorrow she would start to mend the friendship. She'd suggest a mall troll, just the two of them. Maybe with some alone time, Beth would tell her everything. This time, she'd be listening. Cam flipped over on the bed and pressed her cheek to the cool, soft pillow. Maybe if she willed it, sleep would come.

On the other side of the white night table that separated their twin beds, Alex lay awake, her back to Cam. She could hear her twin's brain racing, but refused to tap in. How many times before had she heard this whiny song? So what if Camryn and Beth tripped on a speed bump along the road to lifelong friendship? Big whoop. Tomorrow was all do-over day. Cam believed that.

But Alex checked her scorn. Cam, or Apolla, was sunny-side-up girl, named for the sun god. Was it fair for Alex to be PO'd at her lite take on life, her optimism? It was Cam's nature, probably.

So was it *her* nature to brood? To see the dark side?

Or was that her reality? Last night, in Dave's office, Alex had found her file. The one that held the letter from an attorney representing Isaac Fielding. The one that was now challenging the Barnes' petition of guardianship.

Other papers were there, too. Proof that he had, in fact, been the legal husband of Sara Fielding, and although there were no adoption papers ever found, the man had effectively been Alex's father. The letters went on about some bogus "financial considerations" forcing a separation and his move to another part of the country. But now he was back on his feet and ready to resume his responsibility to the child — especially now that his beloved Sara was gone. Beloved! Alex nearly vomited. He'd done nothing but cause her heartbreak and lead them, she and Sara, down a road her mom would never return from: poverty.

Ike Fielding was a slug, a spineless bottom-feeder.

David Barnes was a righteous man, dedicated to justice. If there *were* any justice in this world, he'd prevail.

There was a glimmer of hope. So far — okay, it had only been a few days — Ike had not responded to the letters and calls from Dave's office summoning him to the hearing.

Timing was everything: If Ike disappeared this time, he'd finally get it right.

Alex could hear the sounds of Cam's breathing. Her

twin had finally fallen asleep. With a little luck, she would, too.

Come with me, Artemis, you are needed.

A man's hushed voice whispered.

Karsh? Is that . . . you? For a minute, Alex didn't know where she was.

Artemis, only you can save her. You alone.

Alex struggled to wake up. She blinked. No one was there, only the sleeping Cam. Who obviously was not hearing what she was.

There isn't much time. Arise, now!

Karsh? It didn't sound like him. The voice was high-pitched, whiny, not raspy and comforting. But who else could it be?

It had to be him! Ileana had freed him, and now he was talking to her, summoning her. Alex was wide awake now. Propped up on her elbows, her heart thudding, she looked out at the moonlit night and listened intently.

This night belongs to you and you alone, Artemis.

If you want to save your friend, you will come — alone. Don't bring Apolla.

The friend? Beth!

Why me? she asked telepathically.

Because, the voice said, *you are a creature of the night, Artemis.*

CHAPTER TWENTY
INTO THE RAVE

Stealth. The word came to Alex as she soundlessly — so as not to awaken her sister — nervously slipped into black leather pants and a black shirt. Her thoughts had been invaded in a stealthlike manner. Now she'd be evading Cam and the entire Barnes clan as she crept out of the house and into the still of the night. Instinctively, she'd reached for her necklace, then remembered she didn't have it.

The voice, Karsh, had told her he'd be waiting for her. In a black car parked around the corner.

Alex's heart was racing. Something was wrong. Why had Karsh sounded so . . . artificial? Had Cam heard anything? She looked over at her twin, sleeping peacefully.

*   *   *

He was waiting just where he said, in a car so big and black, it reminded Alex of a hearse. Shaking off the creeping terror, she opened the door and slowly slid in, profoundly aware of being alone. Without her sister, without her amulet, was she crazy to sneak out in the middle of the night like this?

No. If Karsh had summoned her, there was a crucial reason. If Karsh had called her, she'd be protected.

Only the man behind the wheel wasn't Karsh.

Alex froze.

"Lock the door," he instructed. His voice was sinister as he kept his beady eyes on the road. "We don't want to risk losing you before we even get there."

Fredo. So this was Fredo. Lizard-boy, Cam called him. The idiot uncle, Ileana had said.

Fredo had tricked her.

She regarded his profile. He had a long, thin nose and concave cheeks. Wisps of whiskers grew from a pointy chin. His slicked-back, thinning hair wasn't doing much to cover a balding head. Her uncle. What a pathetic excuse for a man, let alone a supposedly powerful warlock. Dude! Her old slumlord, Hardy Beeson, had been scarier than this weasel!

Alex was no longer afraid. If he were all they could

summon up, she could handle him. "So you tricked me. Score one for you. What's the breaking news?"

"It's simple, my dear . . . niece. The time has come."

"Ditch the warlock mumbo jumbo. The time has come for what?"

He grimaced. Clearly, she wasn't as scared as he'd hoped. "You'll find out everything you need to know soon. Now shut up." He tried to cackle demonically, hoping to scare her. All that came out was a rude snorting sound.

"Soon" stretched into a half hour. Alex was at a double disadvantage. She didn't have Cam's see-in-the-dark peepers, and she wasn't familiar with the streets or back alleys of this town. She had no idea where they were. Worse, Fredo acted like he was in some movie, trying to ditch a phantom tail. He took all these hairpin twists and turns that couldn't have been necessary. The streets of Marble Bay were empty at this hour.

Finally, he pulled to a stop in front of a warehouse on a deserted side street. Alex noticed a scattering of cars on the street, and some bikes, too. The parking lot in back, however, was jammed with cars. And though it wouldn't have been audible to the normal ear, she heard the music, loud, pulsating, trancelike beats of electronica, coming from inside the building.

Entering the cavernous space, Alex thought she might choke. Dark, smoky, and filled with enough sweat-drenched people to exceed the fire limit three times over, it was everything she feared. Pulsating blasts of neon-bright beams of light streaked the room, punctuating the near-complete blackness with the urgency of ambulance flashers.

Beth could be anywhere. It would be easy to be swallowed up by the crowd, lost.

Spinning on her heel, she stuck her finger at a startled Fredo's nose. "Where is she?"

Swiping her finger away, he said evenly, "Don't take that tone with me, niece. . . ."

"Cut the niece crap, you freak. Where's Beth? Is she even here?"

"Oh, she's here. I can assure you of that. You're so smart, you find her!"

Alex almost laughed. What was that? The warlock equivalent of *"nah-nah-nah-nah-nah, I know something you don't know. . . ."*

She surveyed the room. Throngs of people, not much older than herself, were dancing, like one giant centipede. Guys with random piercings, longhairs, and spiked heads, girls with neon hair and glow-in-the-dark tattoos. None of them was Beth. At one point, they all raised their arms, swaying in a trancelike motion. At another, they lifted a random person off the floor and tossed him around, a mosh pit in motion.

Think! Alex cursed her lack of supersight. If only she could see what Cam would be able to!

Listen!

And then she heard it. It cut through the din of the hypnotic beat. A thin, barely there voice of a girl trying to hide her rising panic. "Where's Ms. Webb?" And, "I didn't see anyone from Helping Hands. Are you sure this is the Rave to Save?"

And then another voice, smooth, cajoling, comforting. "Of course it's a fund-raiser. The money they collected at the door will all go to the cause."

Beth — and Shane!

"Why are we in *this* room? Shouldn't we go back out on the dance floor and look for Ms. Webb?"

"Forget Ms. Webb. You've done enough for her. Tonight, I have a special treat for you."

Alex heard Beth's heart thumping — scared, but excited. "A treat? What?"

"There are some people I want you to meet. Important people."

Alex bolted in the direction of their voices. Elbowing her way through the mass of bodies, across the sticky floor, she ran — keenly aware of Fredo on her heel. She heard Beth thinking, *I wonder if he means*

Helping Hands people, or even some of the kids? Not that this would be a place you'd take them . . .

A beefy bodyguard stood outside the door at the other end of the warehouse. Alex stopped short, darted around him, and tried to push open the door. In a flash, bodyguard dude pulled her away. "That's a private room. No one goes in there."

"I'm going," she started.

Fredo smarmily cut in, "Let her in. She's *family.*"

Leaning around her, he pushed the door open.

She saw the boots first, as his legs were propped up on the desk, the soles facing her. The thick-soled black hobnailed boots that had once been used with such force, they'd smashed through the floor of her trailer. They could easily make the sound she'd heard, heavy footsteps stomping down a creaking staircase.

"He's not here."

The voice. Deep and menacing. She looked up. His glinting black eyes were taking her in. Thantos. Uncle Thantos.

"Karsh, the one you're thinking of . . ." The powerful warlock was sitting at a dark wood desk. ". . . is a guest of mine, along with your guardian witch, the talented Ileana. They're in a safe house. Not far from here, actually. But, alas, they won't be making it to our little family reunion."

Alex nearly spit.

"Now, dear sweet Artemis. How. . . ." He rose and looked her up and down. "Why are you dressed like that?"

"Right back atcha," she said defiantly, taking in his long black cape. "Is this vampire night at the rave?"

His throaty laugh, so different from Fredo's goatlike neighing, scared her.

"Touché. What a brave little front you put on — I can't help but feel proud."

Feel this, is what Alex wanted to say, desperately looking around for something to magically throw at his head. She stopped abruptly; he'd know exactly what she was thinking. "Where's Beth?" she demanded.

"Beth?" Thantos sounded puzzled.

Fredo reminded him, "The bait. Artemis's best friend. That's why I brought her first."

Alex was sickened. Uncle Fredo was so dim-witted, he hadn't even known he had the wrong twin.

Now he was saying eagerly, "She's in the back room. Should I bring her out?"

Alex took in her surroundings now. The room, L-shaped, was a posh office, with only one small push-out window high on the wall behind the desk. Two white leather couches flanked an expensive end table, on which sat a potted ficus tree. A door on the far wall probably led to an even more private inner sanctum.

At Thantos's command, Fredo loped over and opened it. "It's time," he said into the room. "One has been delivered."

Shane emerged first — Alex had only seen him once, at the mall, and she was startled by his gentle good looks. Cocoa eyes, tousled light brown hair, smooth skin, and a killer smile. But was that the smile of a killer?

Beth followed tentatively. Wearing a leopard-print tank top and loose-fitting satin pants, she seemed so innocent and confused, mostly. "Alex? What are you doing here?"

"You need to leave," Alex said urgently. "Go home, now!"

Beth turned to Shane. "Why's she here? And are these . . ." She eyed Thantos and Fredo. "The important people you wanted me to meet?"

Alex grabbed Beth's elbow and tried to pull her toward the door. But Shane moved to block the way. "I'll take Beth home," he said, "when Lord Thantos instructs me to."

"Lord Thantos? What's he lord of?" Beth laughed, nervously scratching at her arm.

"Lord is my title," Thantos told her. "It means I have earned a certain rank, the highest in my *peer* group."

Shane added, "It's an honor to have been of service.

And since Miss Fish has fulfilled her role, if it pleases you, sir, I'll take her home now."

"My role?" Beth asked nervously. "Of service? What are you talking about?"

"They used you," Alex spat out bitterly, "to get to me."

Beth's dark eyes flashed angrily — at Alex. "The apple never falls far from the twin tree. At the core, you both think everything's about you!"

Shane slipped his arm around Beth's waist and began to lead her toward the door.

Thantos boomed, "You are correct. She *has* fulfilled her role. Now dispose of her."

Alex's heart began to pound.

Beth's knees buckled. She would have fallen, had Shane not been holding her.

Shane was stunned. "What?"

"What part of 'dispose of her' don't you understand?" Thantos said matter-of-factly. "Knock her out with the prescribed herbs, take her somewhere, and dispose of her. It's quite simple, really. Quite doable, as you young people say."

Shane turned ashen. "With all due respect, my lord, you never said anything about that. She's an innocent bystander. She's nothing to you."

"Exactly! She's served her purpose. She brought Aron's daughter to me. I don't need her anymore."

Alex frantically looked around the room. The plant! She closed her eyes — but Fredo grabbed her by the shoulders and turned her around. "Don't even think about it, little niece," he warned. "Your kiddie-pool powers are no match for us. You're playing in the grown-up pool now. The deep end — and you can't swim."

Beth's body began to wrack with sobs. Alex threw Fredo's hands off her and dashed over, positioning herself between the frightened girl and Thantos. "Let her go. It's me you want."

Thantos's thick eyebrows went up. "How selfless."

"I mean it," Alex declared. "Spare her, take me."

The hulking warlock shot her a twisted smile. "Maybe I will — but it's not you alone I want." And then he winked!

"Never!" Alex fought to not think the words, but she couldn't stop herself. *Don't communicate with Cam. Don't tell her where we are.*

Thantos deftly read her mind. "You won't have to. Where you go, your sister will follow. She's probably on her way now."

She had to warn Cam. *Don't come! It's a trap!*

"Too late."

She heard him, but the sound of his evil laughter

now came at her as if through earmuffs. The room started to get fuzzy. Shane, lightning quick, bolted out the door. Coward!

And that horrible freaky Fredo came toward her, tossing some powder in her face.

That was the last thing Alex saw before her world went black. Her last thought, screamed as loudly as she could, was to her sister. *Don't come! It's a trap!*

CHAPTER TWENTY-ONE
FRIENDS TILL THE END

Cam bolted upright in bed, drenched in sweat. Her head was pounding; an icy chill swirled around her, making her teeth chatter. She'd been dreaming. First she was flying, then she was falling. And something was gone, missing. She felt for her sun necklace, but no — she knew where that was.

Alex!

In a panic, she threw off the covers and leaped over to the other bed. It was empty, but for a lump of crunched-up covers. She ran to the bathroom, although she knew she wouldn't find her twin there — or downstairs in the kitchen, either. She just *knew*. Alex wasn't home. And Alex was in trouble.

Where are you? Where did you go?

She opened the window and stared directly into the full moon. Her eyes started to sting. She saw a dark room, a mass of people, flashing neon lights. The rave? Was Alex at the rave?

Closing the window quietly, she quickly dressed in the outfit she'd tossed on the floor from yesterday. Think! Think! Als was at the rave, but where was it? Why'd she go without me? And how could I have slept through Alex's hasty exit?

Would she ever be able to hear as well as Alex could?

Thump! Was she hearing things now? She spun around. The window had opened! By itself? Cam thought she was going crazy, until she saw what had made the sound: A pair of legs swung over the sill into her room, then arms, a torso, attached to . . . Shane?

"What are you doing here?" she demanded anxiously.

"Shhh . . . you'll wake everyone up. Hurry — we've got to go."

And Cam knew. Bad guy or good guy or whatever he was, Shane was here to take her to Alex. For better or for worse.

He explained little on the way there. And later, Cam couldn't be sure of exactly *how* they'd gotten there. Had they really flown? Or was that part of her dream?

She was completely clear about everything that happened the minute Shane led her into the warehouse. Together, they'd pushed through the mass of people, who all seemed to move to one beat. They blasted past the guard, through the door in the far corner of the room.

Slumped on the couch were the limp bodies of two people Cam loved.

Alex. Her other half.

And Beth. Her best friend.

Her friend till the end. But the end wasn't supposed to come now.

Her hand flew to her mouth. She spun, enraged — now face-to-face with both of them. Fredo and Thantos. Her uncles. In the Olympics of family dysfunction, did they not get the gold?

Thantos, black-bearded, hulking, and massive, was sitting at a desk, arms clasped behind his head, long legs propped up on it. He'd been waiting for her.

Fredo hadn't. Or at least, he seemed surprised to see her with Shane. Still, he took the credit. "The other one has come. Delivered. You see, brother, I emerge triumphant. You doubted me, but I prevailed in the end."

"Indeed you did." Thantos's stare bore into Cam and she began to feel dizzy. "But it was I who commissioned the boy. Shane." Thantos eyed him warily. "I see you've fulfilled your duty in spite of doubting me. You will be re-warded. Go now, back to Coventry Island."

But Shane stood rooted.

Thantos turned his attention back to Cam. "Apolla, my dear. I'm thrilled you've decided to join us. It's the right thing to do."

But Cam was no longer looking at him. Trembling with fear, she walked slowly over to Alex. Was she breathing? Was Beth?

A sudden knock at the door startled her. It seemed to surprise Thantos, Fredo, and Shane, too, who jumped.

"Expecting anyone?" Thantos boomed at the two of them.

"Of course not!" Fredo insisted. Shane shook his head.

The door opened, and the bodyguard walked in, carrying a three-foot-high brass statue, an elaborate sculpture of a winged cat.

"What is that?" Thantos demanded. "I said, no inter-ruptions."

The bodyguard shrugged. "I'm sorry, Mr. Sot Naht, but the owners of this warehouse, or whatever, ordered this. I wouldn't let the delivery guys bring it in. But it looks like it might be worth big bucks. I wouldn't want it to be stolen."

"Oh, just put it down and get out!" Thantos boomed, with a wave of his massive arm.

The bodyguard gingerly put the statue on the floor, ducked out quickly, and closed the door.

"Now, where were we? Oh, yes, I was telling you how pleased I am that you showed up for our family reunion. I knew you would."

"What did you do to them? Are they . . . okay?" Cam asked shakily, her back still to him.

Thantos sounded exasperated. "The friend is of no use to me. But why would I harm your sister? Or you? I merely want to return you to the family you've been stolen from. To give you, to share with you, what is rightfully yours."

Cam turned slowly around. She felt herself soothed by his voice. And she wanted to know more. "Where's my mother — ?"

Turn away! Don't let him connect with your eyes! Have I taught you nothing? The voice — was it Ileana's?

A sudden blast of wind banged the window above the desk shut, breaking her connection with Thantos. Cam instantly felt clearheaded. She yelled, "Shane! Hurry — get Beth!"

The boy bounded into action. Before Thantos or Fredo could react, he lifted the sleeping Beth off the couch, and bolted out the door with her.

"Get Apolla!" Thantos thundered at Fredo.

Instead of reciting a spell, turning her into a stone or a pebble, Fredo lunged toward her. Flashback! Just as he had during the dance. Cam almost laughed, it was so déjà vu all over again. Could she? Would he fall for it again?

She faked to the left, then spun to the right — ducking under his arm! She dashed toward the door, frantically looking for some weapon, something she could use against him.

A hand clamped onto her shoulder hard. "Come, come, Apolla," Thantos warned. "You can't possibly think you can win against the two of us. We're much more powerful than you. Alone as you seem to be."

"That's where you're wrong. On two counts. She's not helpless. And she's not alone."

Thantos's powerful hand dropped from Cam's shoulder. He turned slowly. The statue of the cat was moving somehow, stretching upward and outward, its features reforming into a woman. Shape-shifting into Ileana. There was fire in her eyes. And a look of sweet satisfaction on her face.

Fredo took a step toward her, but Thantos reached out to stop him. "I'll handle this."

"Well, well. So you managed to get free. Very clever. I'm proud of you. And shape-shifting into a statue, getting yourself delivered into my lair! So much more clever than that paltry pigeon morph you did earlier. I'm practically bursting with pride."

"It's your ego that needs bursting," Ileana sniped. "Let the twins go."

"Go? Away from me? They don't want to, right, Apolla? Look at me."

A part of Cam wanted to. She looked up, about to lock eyes with the one who had such power over her, who could take her to her —

She heard Karsh. *Don't be lured. Remember who you are. Aron's daughter would not fall into this trap. Keep your eyes on Ileana.*

Cam swung around — just in time to see it come flying her way. Her sun necklace, Ileana had tossed it to her. Her hand closed around it. And she felt the familiar tingle, the warmth radiating from it, heard the humming. She focused on Ileana, whose delicate hand wrapped around Alex's moon charm.

Could this work? For her and Ileana?

Thantos threw his head back and snickered. "You're going to try and use magick against me? Against . . . us? Wait, allow me to sit down. This should be quite the show." He backed into the chair behind the desk.

Ileana walked over to Cam and opened her palm.

Turning toward the unconscious Alex, she began the incantation.

Arise, Artemis, stand and fight!

Succumb not to the herb that closes your eyes to light.

Cam unfisted her hand. She held on to the chain — and watched, entranced, as her sun charm moved on its own, as if magnetized, toward Alex's moon charm. If the two fused, as they did when she and Alex used them, would they have a chance against Thantos?

Together we three against evil prevail, Ileana was still chanting.

Together, the forces of good cannot fail.

It happened! The amulets found each other and fused together.

Thantos sat back, amused. Cam thought she saw Alex's eyelids flutter. Was it working? And then it happened. The plant from the table, the big potted ficus tree, suddenly went careening across the room, bopping the shocked Fredo on the head.

It didn't knock him out. It only enraged him.

Ooops.

It didn't take a premonition for Cam and Alex to know what was about to happen. Fredo was going to do what he'd done before — even though it hadn't worked then and probably wouldn't now. Cam almost wanted to say, "Fangs for the memories."

The shape of the goatlike man stretched up and out, his thin skin popping into scales, sharp teeth growing into long fangs — turning into the giant lizard again! Its sharp, yellow talons lunged for them. Only Ileana blocked his path, kicking him in his scaly stomach, stopping him.

Thantos bolted up furiously and pushed his face into Cam's. "You dare defy me?" Cam's eyes began to sting as his glittering black eyes pinned her. She thought she'd pass out.

Ileana, trying to hold Fredo back, shouted, "Turn away! Cover your eyes!"

Alex had been waiting for her moment. Now! Fully awake and powered up, she dove onto the floor and grabbed Thantos's ankle with both hands, intent on tripping him. She did it — but just before the great warlock went down, he sent another bolt of eye-lightning at Cam, who was flung backward just as Fredo was advancing.

The impact of Cam flying through the air knocked the giant lizard off balance. Eight hundred pounds of ugly, scaly monster fell on top of Thantos. Pinning him to the floor.

Ileana yelled at the twins, "Go now! Get away from here."

Cam stood firm. "Not without you."

Ileana whirled around. "Don't argue with me! I am your guardian and I command you to leave. This instant!"

But the twins ignored her command. "Did you free Karsh?" Cam had to know.

"Did the necklaces help?" Alex hoped they had.

"Is he okay?"

"Where is he?"

Exasperated, Ileana shouted, "You ask too many questions! But . . ." She softened. "If you must know. Yes, I did free him." She stopped, bit her lip, and focused her amazing gray eyes on them. "But I didn't do it alone. You helped. The necklaces helped."

"And?" Cam was only half teasing.

"And what?" Ileana, annoyed again, demanded.

"And don't you want to say, 'Thank you, Alexandra and Camryn'? 'I couldn't have done it without —'"

Fed up, Ileana grabbed both twins by their elbows and forced them through the door. "We are out of here! Now!"

The T*Witches and their guardian raced through the crowd. They were almost to the exit when they heard it. A groundswell of screams and shrieks filled the warehouse and then, "Lizard boy! Go! Lizard boy, go!"

What the — ?? They whirled around. The sight that met their eyes was one they'd never forget. Thantos, who'd obviously managed to free himself, wildly searching the dance floor for them. And Fredo — caught mid-morph between species, the top half a man, the bottom half still a lizard — being hoisted up by the crowd and tossed around, like a cucumber in a salad. Fredo was in the mosh pit. The ravers thought he was the coolest thing they'd ever seen.

CHAPTER TWENTY-TWO
WHERE WE BELONG

Shane was waiting for them when they got home. The fierce young warlock was in their room, sitting cross-legged on the carpet, noodling with Alex's guitar.

He'd left the window open. Cam let a small smile escape. "We have to stop meeting like this. Someone's going to suspect something."

Alex plopped down on the floor next to him and gently took the guitar away. "Waking the family is probably not the move."

He smiled sheepishly. "Right. I forgot — it's still dark outside."

"Beth — is she okay?" Cam settled into the swivel chair and hugged her knees.

Shane looked up at her. "She's fine — sorry, I should have said that right away. I took her home; she's sleeping now. The skullcap herbs wear off after a while — "

"Even without a counter spell," Alex said.

Shane asked, "That's how you came out of it so quickly?"

"That and a little help from our parents." Alex's hand closed around her moon necklace, now safely back on her neck. "Did you know them?"

Shane shook his head. "No. I was only a kid when . . . well, it happened. But I heard about it, of course. It was the talk of Coventry Island."

Alex touched his arm. "If you knew Lord Thantos was responsible for their deaths, why would you work for him?"

Shane took his time before responding, keenly aware of the unnerving stares of both twins. "Like many warlocks of my age, I grew up believing Lord Thantos had been unfairly accused. When he asked for my help, I was honored. He said you'd been stolen when you were infants, and he wanted to bring you back. After tonight, I don't know what to think. Except what a fool I've been. I was so easily duped."

"But in the clutch, you came through. You saved Beth's life," Cam reminded him gently.

"You did a one-eighty. We owe you," Alex added.

He grinned, and Cam couldn't help it. Her tummy

actually did a flip-flop. "I think it's the other way around," the washboard-ab boy said. "No, I owe you — at least an explanation."

Alex sprang up. "Wait! We have a rule. No confession sessions without —"

"Snacks!" Cam finished her twin's thought. "There's munchies and juice, or iced tea in the —"

Alex waved her off. "I know where everything is. I live here, too, you know."

They stayed up until dawn. Shane told them what he knew. The most crucial fact: Thantos had told him to capture Cam, knowing Alex would follow.

"And the Helping Scam-o-rama, where'd that fit in?" Alex wanted to know.

"Dumb luck," Shane said, munching on Emily's homemade trail mix. "I needed a way to lure Cam. I started at the mall. Your hangout."

Alex playfully punched her sis. "I told you being a mall crawler would come to no good."

Cam rolled her eyes. "Continue."

"I came across the Helping Hands cart and looked into it. I found out right away it was a scam, but it was a convincing scam. So I signed up, figuring I'd use it to make contact with you, get you to trust me."

"And if I hadn't crashed into you that day?" Cam asked.

"I'd have gotten your attention somehow." He winked. He had a curious mix of self-confidence and modesty that was hard to resist.

Alex held up her hand. "Back up. Why'd you target her with the Helping Hands thing? Why not me? Or whichever one you met first?"

Shane shrugged. "She's idealistic, more likely to be drawn to a cause like that."

"And what am I, cynical twin?" Alex was only half-kidding.

"You're more suspicious. It's your nature," Shane said. "It would have been harder to lure you."

"Actually?" Alex owned her bad. "This time, Cam was skeptical girl. She knew something was rotten in the state of Cause-ville. I kept insisting she was overreacting."

Cam said thoughtfully, "How do you know so much about us?"

"Lord Thantos knows everything. About you, your friends — and your family."

Cam and Alex shuddered in tandem.

"I almost had you that day at the mall," Shane said, "but then Beth showed up and you had that fight with her. I knew she was your best friend, so I revised the plan."

"You used her instead," Cam said regretfully, "to get to me."

Alex reminded Cam, "He saved her instead."

"You do like her, a little?" Cam said tentatively. "It wasn't all just a big act?"

Shane fished a note out of his pocket and folded it in half. "Will you give her this when you see her? I never meant to hurt her. Beth is smart and caring. When she believes in something, there's no stopping her."

Alex voiced what the twins were thinking. "Thantos. Would you stop at anything for him? Would you kill for him?"

Shane's gaze was sad and soulful. "I couldn't have answered that question before tonight. Maybe. I don't know. But being around the two of you changed everything. It reminded me of something. And it hit me hard."

"What's that?" Cam asked.

Shane ticked off the reasons on his fingers. "You didn't grow up among us on Coventry Island. You didn't even grow up together, or know you were witches. But instinctively, you saw a wrong and tried to right it. You did everything to save an innocent from harm. Even at the risk of your own lives. Seeing you two in action was like a kick in the butt. That's what *our kind* do. And that's not what Thantos was doing."

"What will you do now?" Cam asked quietly, basking in the glow of Shane's heartfelt words.

He stretched his long legs and got up. "Go home. To Coventry Island."

"But is it safe there? Didn't you just make Thantos's Most Wanted list?"

"After tonight, I'm probably not safe anywhere," Shane admitted. "But my family's there, my friends. And the Unity Council. I'm honor-bound to report what happened tonight. Anyway, Coventry Island is where I belong."

Is it where we belong, too? Alex thought, but didn't say aloud.

She didn't have to. Shane answered, "That's a decision you will have to make for yourselves. When the time comes."

And then he was gone.

The twins were too fried to go to school the next day. Cam straggled downstairs in the morning, telling her parents they both were grappling with "some stomach thing." Neither Dave nor, surprisingly, Emily, pushed it.

When they did get up, well after noon, the house was empty. Emily left a note saying she was at a client's house, measuring for drapes.

As soon as she showered and had breakfast, Cam

e-mailed Beth, asking to hang out after school. *I haven't been the greatest friend,* she wrote, *but I know what happened last night. And I have a message from Shane. Meet me at Half Moon Cove at five — Bethie, I have a lot to tell you. Please.*

Next, she called Dave at the office for an update on Webb and Lizzie.

Her dad sounded relieved to hear from her. "So you're both feeling better?" he asked more than once.

"We're fine," Cam assured him. "It's been a kind of roller-coaster week — and it's only halfway through."

"Well, I'm glad you called, princess," Dave said. "We've had a hectic but pretty good morning. Is Alex there? I want you both to hear this."

Not only had Cecilia Webb been taken into custody, but the police, working off Lizzie's information, were on the way to breaking open the entire scam. "Helping Hands is definitely a front for a ring of thieves," Dave told them.

"Led by Webb?" Cam guessed.

"Led by Sam Rogers," Dave corrected her, "husband of Belinda Rogers."

"Who happens to reside in the state penitentiary?" Alex guessed.

There was a pause. Dave obviously wanted to know how Alex and Cam came by that info — but he never did ask. Instead, he told them, "Samuel Rogers is doing ten to fifteen years for robbery and endangering the welfare of a minor. He claimed he'd been set up by his cronies, who were just as guilty. His wife, Belinda — Ms. Webb, that is — knew she'd be next. So she was frantically trying to get enough money to run from the gang, and maybe start fresh. Anyway, the scheme was to keep on the move, luring at-risk kids into stealing for them, under the guise of doing good."

Cam was upset. "That's horrible."

"So they've done this before, and no one got caught?" Alex said.

"They chose their victims well," Dave explained. "Only kids whose parents weren't likely to investigate and put the brakes on. Pretty clever."

"And Lizzie, is she okay?" Cam asked.

"Thanks to both of you, she's off the hook, safe at home."

With no Helping Hands meeting or soccer practice to go to, Beth had come straight home from school. And to Cam's relief, logged on and read the e-mail right away. Best of all, she agreed to meet at Half Moon Cove. Where, Cam hoped, they'd take the first steps toward patching their fractured friendship.

"I wish I could tell her everything — the whole truth," she fretted to Alex before she left.

"You won't have to. At the risk of going all 'Sunday night TV movie' on you, tell her what's in your heart. That'll be enough," Als counseled. "Oh, and one more thing —"

"Covered," Cam said with a knowing smile. "One quart of Ben & Jerry's Chunky Monkey, two spoons."

"*Two* spoons? And they call you selfish!" Alex teased. "Yo, you've got a friendship to repair. Bounce!"

CHAPTER TWENTY-THREE
THE BITTERSWEET TRUTH

Beth was waiting when Cam got there. Hungry for a download — and, to Cam's relief, for ice cream, too. "About last night," her friend started, holding her palm out for a spoon, "how could you know what happened? You weren't even there."

"I actually was — later. And I always suspected that something was" — she poked Beth in the ribs — "pardon the expression, *fishy* . . . about Helping Hands, but it took a while before I figured out the real deal."

The bulletin that Helping Hands was a scam didn't shock Beth, not after the rave. "Was that a surreal scene, or what?"

Cam, spooning ice cream into her mouth, agreed. "Raves in our sleepy little hamlet. Who knew?"

"The whole thing feels like one weird dream." Beth shook her head. "I even dreamed that someone wanted to kill me. Over-the-top much?"

Cam bit down on the spoon. And let it slide.

But Beth remembered Thantos and Fredo. "Who *were* those people?"

"They're the bad guys, Bethie," was all Cam had to say.

Beth rushed on, "Bad guys — like Ms. Webb. I trusted her! I worked so hard for her. What a total lamebrain I was."

"You weren't alone on the lamebrain train. At least one really cute guy was right there with you, if it makes you feel any better."

"Shane. Mr. Wright. Mr. *Yeah, right,*" Beth said sarcastically.

Cam pulled Shane's note out of her jeans pocket and handed it to Beth. "A message from the aforementioned Mr. Wright. I don't know what he wrote, but he really is okay. You weren't wrong to trust him."

Beth couldn't hide a half-smile. Or the blush creeping up her neck. "Uh, I think I'll open it later. First, tell me how you found out about the whole scam."

Cam dug deep into the creamy dessert. "It was a clever plan — full of half-truths. Sunshine House really *is* what they said it was. Unfortunately, you weren't raising money for it." When Cam told her about Lizzie, Beth was shocked. She hadn't been asked to steal anything. So far.

"So your mother's necklace —"

"Mom found it. She totally forgot she'd put it in the vault for safekeeping. She's been a little frazzled lately. But now I understand why you thought I took it."

"I never should have doubted you, that's so my bad. I *know* you, Elisabeth Ellen Fish, and you would never do that, no matter what."

"No matter what, huh? Who'd have thought I could be so easily tricked? I really believed we were doing something good, something important," Beth said mournfully. "How stupid was I?"

"Not stupid! Just hurting."

Beth searched Cam's face. "You know?"

"Sort of. I know bad stuff is happening at home."

Beth swallowed, fighting back tears.

"And instead of being there for you, I totally turned my back. Butt-ugly truth alert . . ." Cam paused and sucked in her breath. "You were right. It never, for one *second,* occurred to me that it *wasn't* about me, that you weren't still just bummed about the Alex thing. I messed up. If you let me fix . . . ?"

A teardrop slid down Beth's freckled cheek. "So you know about my parents?"

Cam had brought tissues. "Some. Ready to hear more. If you want."

"They're always fighting. It's like if my mom says one thing, my dad contradicts it, even if it's just some stupid small thing. And then my mom argues, or she'll get all sulky and quiet. Or my dad walks out. Finally, yesterday they told me and Lauren they were having problems. They're going to try some counseling thing. But if it doesn't work" — Beth's voice cracked — "they'll probably separate."

Cam put her arm around Beth, who rested her frizzy head on Cam's shoulder. "You must be so scared," she said gently.

"It's like they've already decided. Like the counseling thing is just some sort of exercise."

"You never know," Cam said evenly. "If they have a good therapist, it could work out. I know from my dad's practice — they handle lots of divorce cases — that at least half the time, it actually does work out. Your parents have a lot of good years between them. A whole history, not to mention two extremely fabulous daughters. There are bumps in the road of all relationships."

"Even ours," Beth conceded. "At least we're sorta back on track."

"Sorta?! What's this sorta stuff?" Cam playfully nudged Beth off her shoulder. "Friends —"

"Till the end!" Luckily, Beth didn't notice Cam shudder when they locked pinkies.

While Cam was off mending fences, Alex was mending a song she'd started. She tinkered with Dylan's guitar — which now really did feel like hers — trying out lyrics and chords. It was cool that the whole Helping Scams thing was busted, but Dave had not said anything about Ike. Had he still not heard, or had Ike responded and Dave not wanted to tell her?

"Positive thoughts, send positive karma out there." That's what Amanda would say now. "It'll come back to you." Alex liked Amanda.

"Face your fears head-on." That's probably what Sukari would say. "And make a plan." She liked that girl, too.

"Oh, just hire a good lawyer. You can buy your way out of having to go with the evil stepmonster." Alex could practically hear Brianna in her head.

The next sound she heard wasn't in her head. The front door slammed so hard, it rocked the house — and not in a good way! The argument, apparently, had been in progress awhile.

"How could you do that? Aside from everything

else, you embarrassed me — I get a call at a client's house, come to the principal's office to get you!?"

Emily. Offended *and* on the offense.

"Sorry to mess up your day, but it's no big deal."

Dylan. Guilty, sulky, defensive.

Alex tensed. She knew the reason for their moods and their 'tudes.

"What's going on with you?" Emily was now pacing the kitchen. "It isn't bad enough that you're dropping out of everything. Now you're smoking! What are you trying to prove?"

Alex could hear Dylan slump into a chair. She pictured him propping his elbows up on the table, head down, running his hands through his hair. "You're making a big deal out of nothing. So what if I'm sick of basketball? And everyone smokes, so I tried a couple of lousy cigarettes. I'm not trying to prove anything. I'm just being me."

Alex ached. She'd failed him. She'd caught him smoking at school a few days ago and made him stop. But she wasn't in school today. And he'd gotten caught.

"Being *you*? Listen to me, Dylan Michael Barnes. *You* don't smoke. And that's all there is to it."

"You don't even know me," Dylan whined.

Emily gritted her teeth. "All I have to know is this. Nicotine is a drug. And as long as you're under this roof,

221

you will not smoke. Now, go to your room. You're grounded."

"For how long?"

"Indefinitely!"

Alex heard Dylan drag himself up the stairs. And she knew better than to go down to the kitchen, where Emily would be fuming. But she couldn't help it. Her sister had *dared* her to break into Emily's head. Well, this seemed like the primo moment. Okay, Ems was freaking — with good reason! But Alex needed to know, did Emily blame her?

She found Dylan's mom on the phone with Dave, asking if he could come home now. She didn't tell him why, but hung up, apparently satisfied that he was on his way.

"Hi," Alex tried to sound casual.

Emily was startled. "What are you doing — oh, I forgot you were home today." Tense, she asked if she and Cam were feeling better, but what Alex heard was not concern for her health. *I just bet this is her influence. He's done nothing but defy me since she got here. And now this!*

"You're wrong," Alex said. "For one thing, I had nothing to do with Dylan's decision. He doesn't confide in me, and even if he did, I wouldn't tell him to drop out of sports. No matter what you think, I'm not turning your son against you."

Emily brushed away her bangs, flustered. "How did you . . . ? I'm not blaming you."

"But that's what you're thinking. It's written all over your face," Alex improvised.

Emily whirled on her, her voice loud now. "Tell me you didn't know he was smoking!"

"I did know that. But —"

Dylan came flying down the stairs and rushed into the kitchen. He'd heard. "Mom! Wait. This is bogus. Be mad at me all you want, but you're wrong about Alex."

Emily's eyebrows arched. "You don't need to protect her."

"Mom!" Dylan was more upset now than he'd been before. "You don't understand! Alex tried to make me stop. When she found out I was smoking, dude, she went medieval on me. She follows me everywhere at school — she's like the butt police. She's totally in my face. It's like this obsession with her."

Her mother! Oh, my god, her mother died of cancer. I wonder if it was — Emily's hand flew to her mouth.

Quietly, Alex told her, "Lung cancer. It was lung cancer. And yes, she was addicted to cigarettes."

Dylan awkwardly wrapped his arms around Alex. "Sorry for playing the dead-mother card that first day when you went postal on me. That was totally out of line."

Tears welled up in Emily's swimming-pool-blue

eyes. Alex heard her thinking, *I thought I was trying to be a good mother, to accept her. But look what I did — just because she's different from us, and sarcastic, I assumed she was a bad influence on him.* Out loud, she said, "Alex, I'm so sorry."

Cam and her dad ended up getting home at the same time, walking in on Emily sobbing quietly and Dylan hugging Alex.

"Is this a very special episode of *7th Heaven*?" Dave quipped. "Tell me it's nothing worse."

Emily, wiping away tears, explained everything.

Dave went into default lawyer mode. "Any other witnesses?" He looked at Alex, who shook her head. And his son, who said, "Mom pretty much got it all."

"Okay, then," he said, adjusting his bifocals on the bridge of his nose.

"I've made my decision. A) Dylan. You're not smoking. That's nonnegotiable. And B) We're a family. We make mistakes, we misjudge one another, and sometimes say hurtful things. But in the end, we do what's right for one another. Thank you, Alex, for trying to do that."

Cam asked the question Alex was afraid to. "What about Isaac Fielding? Is the hearing set up?"

Dave's face brightened. "Postponed. Indefinitely. He hasn't responded to our letters, faxes, or e-mails, either through his lawyer or on his own. So for now, we keep moving forward."

"Dude, I like the sound of that." Dylan joked, "I'll get started building the cupboard below the staircase —"

Alex kicked Dylan. "I'll get started waving my magic wand every time I even *think* you're thinking about a cigarette. I am gonna be in your face, Dudley."

"I'm counting on it, Harry."

Emily laughed. "I have no idea what you're talking about. I guess I'll have to read the book."

"Great idea! Do that instead of cooking." Ooops. The words came flying out of Cam before she realized she'd said it aloud. She quickly backpedaled. "I mean, you know, it's not like you have to cook every night."

Emily grinned sheepishly. "It's pretty . . . suckola, isn't that your word?"

Cam put her arms around her mom.

Alex stood there, inches from them, rolling her eyes at the sappy moment. Suddenly, Emily and Cam, as if they'd had the same idea at the exact same time, reached out to her.

Reluctantly, Alex stepped into their embrace and joined the hug fest.

Emily pulled away only to say, "Grab a chair. This kitchen table fits our family — of five. Perfectly.

CHAPTER TWENTY-FOUR
UNDER THE SACRED TREE

There was a place, the highest point in Mariner's Park, where Cam had been going for many years. The park itself was in the center of the historic district of town, and the spot, one Cam had claimed a long time ago. Or had it claimed her? She'd been almost magnetically drawn to it, though it wasn't more than a scraggly patch of green under an ancient elm tree. Sitting under it gave her a dazzling, unobstructed view of the Marble Bay harbor. And she liked to gaze out at the boats, at the water. Cam had never told anyone about going there. It was her place to write, to think, to daydream, to plot, sometimes even to cry.

Alex was the first, and only, person she'd ever shared it with.

On one of the last days of late autumn, when the air was ripe with the scent of snow, Cam and Alex headed there together. A little more than a week had passed since the rave, since they'd busted open the Helping Hands ring of thieves, since Beth and Cam had made up — and since they'd seen or heard from Thantos, Fredo, Karsh, or Ileana.

Alex felt the wind in her hair as she pedaled next to her twin, through Cam's stately suburban neighborhood. It was so neat and antiseptic. What was *she* doing here?

Once, Alex had said to Cam, "You're acting like you can just cut and paste me into your perfect little life. Well, you can't."

Yet that was exactly what was happening.

And it didn't totally suck.

The twins turned onto the main road that led into town, then circled through the narrow winding streets that gave way to the cobblestones of "old town, Marble Bay." They locked their bikes outside the stand by the arched entrance to the park and without a word or signal raced each other up the winding path that led to their tree.

Alex got there first, half a second ahead of Cam. She pinged Cam's shoulder. "Dude, I beat you."

"Gloat not, *dude,*" Cam mimicked. "I totally let you win. It's all part of the new, unselfish Camryn Barnes."

"Delude yourself much? I *am* the faster twin!" Alex plopped on the ground and Cam settled in beside her.

"Yet you're not so fast on the uptake news. 'Cause I don't think you heard this —" Cam's eyes glinted mischievously.

"The uptake news? What are you, the new Brianna?"

"Well, it was Bree who called. But 'Our Lady of the Satellite Dish' knew *what* happened, but not why."

"Okay, I'll play," Alex said, plucking a blade of grass. "You're busting to tell me — go for it."

"*Who*: Brice Stanley, magnanimous movie star. *What*: donated a ton of money. *To*: Sunshine House! And sista-clone, I think you know why!!"

Alex's majestic eyes widened. "You think?"

"Think! Duh! We probably totally shamed him into doing it."

"But how?" Alex asked. "That little e-mail exchange between Sunshine House and uh . . . Brice . . . was confidential."

"E-mails? Confidential? If you're gonna be a lawyer's daughter, you've got a lot to learn, cybernaif. A) No such thing as confidential e-mails, and B) Ever hear the word *leak*? When Sunshine House heard from deep-pocketed, good-hearted Brice, they probably leaked it to the press. And then how would it look for pricey Bricey to do a U-turn? Can you say, 'Stinko publicity'? His handlers probably told him it was cheaper to make the donation, even if he was sorta scammed into it."

"So in the end," Alex said, "Helping Hands — with an assist by a couple of T*Witches — did really help Sunshine House. I'd call *that* majorly unselfish."

"Whoo-*hoo*! I *am* the unselfish twin!" Cam raised her arms triumphantly.

Alex couldn't help herself. "Yeah, I wonder if Uncle Thantos is up on your personality change."

Cam's smile faded. "Thanks. I needed that. Can't be too happy, can we?"

"Sorry. It just freaked me when Shane said that Thantos knows everything about us."

Especially since he'll be back. Cam shuddered, knowing Alex was reading her mind. She stuck out her chin defiantly. "Just let him! Every day, we get stronger."

Alex slumped against the tree. "Right, keep the faith."

Instinctively, Cam and Alex touched their sun and moon charms, which hung securely around their necks.

"Ileana said she used our necklaces to free Karsh.

So that would mean they work for people besides us," Cam ventured.

"For relatives, that would make sense," Alex agreed.

"So," Cam said it, "you're pretty certain she's — well, because of the eyes, I guess." *But she's not our mother. . . .*

Alex was on the train. *No way.* She shrugged. "Older sister?"

Thoughtfully, Cam said, "Maybe she's not related. Maybe these charms work for anyone, if you're trying to do something good. And maybe lots of people on, uh, Coventry Island have the same weird eyes as us. How would we know, we've never been there."

They stared out at the harbor in silence, for how long they didn't really know. Then, jarringly, Cam's watch beeped. She jumped, almost forgetting why she'd set it.

Alex reminded her, "Something's going on chez Barnes — hadn't we better be getting back?"

Cam gently smacked her palm against her forehead. "Emily's birthday. Party going on."

"Emily?" Alex said. "Don't you mean Mom?"

Cam searched Alex's face for even a hint of sarcasm. She found none.

"She's not only pretty good at the mom thing, she's all we've got," Alex added.

"I don't know," Cam said slowly. "It doesn't seem

like anyone really knows what happened to Miranda. She just vanished."

"Listen to me," Alex said earnestly, "I know something about moms. And so do you. If Miranda were alive, she would have contacted us by now — Sara or Emily would have. They'd have gone to the ends of the earth and beyond to find us, they'd —"

But Cam tuned out. She couldn't help it. Her head suddenly began to throb, and she felt so cold, her teeth chattered. She shut her eyes against the stinging sensation. And Camryn saw:

A room, bathed in sunlight so bright no one without supersight could have seen what was in it. A woman was staring out a big window. Her hair, a dark chestnut color, was braided down her back. And then there were colors! A kaleidoscope of brilliant shades, vibrant patches . . . a quilt? Was she clutching a quilt?

"Als?" Cam grabbed her sister's hand hard.

"What?" Alex held tight, her knuckles white.

"I feel it. I know it. She's alive."

ABOUT THE AUTHORS

H.B. Gilmour is the author of numerous best-selling books for adults and young readers, including the *Clueless* movie novelization and series; *Pretty in Pink,* a University of Iowa Best Book for Young Readers; and *Godzilla,* a Nickelodeon Kids Choice nominee. She also cowrote the award-winning screenplay *Tag*.

H.B. lives in upstate New York with her husband, John Johann, and their misunderstood dog, Fred, one of the family's five pit bulls, three cats, two snakes (a boa constrictor and a python), and five extremely bright, animal-loving children.

Randi Reisfeld has written many best-sellers, such as the *Clueless* series; the *Moesha* series; and biographies of Prince William, New Kids on the Block, and Hanson. Her Scholastic paperback *Got Issues Much?* was named an ALA Best Book for Reluctant Readers in 1999.

Randi has always been fascinated with the randomness of life. . . . About how any of our lives can simply "turn on a dime" and instantly (snap!) be forever changed. About the power each one of us has deep inside, if only we knew how to access it. About how any of us would react if, out of the blue, we came face-to-face with our exact double.

From those random fascinations, T*Witches was born.

Oh, and BTW: She has no twin (that she knows of) but an extremely cool family and cadre of BFFs to whom she is totally devoted.